HAMLET

- Deluxe Edition -

William Shakespeare

GOLDEN CLASSICS

Published by GOLDEN CLASSICS

Black and White Line Drawings by H. C. Selous

TABLE OF CONTENTS

INTRODUCTION

According to countless eminent literary critics, no one like Shakespeare has managed to change us before and after him, just as no one has managed to create, in his works, exemplars of humanity and ID equally autonomous. According to many others, judging a Shakespeare's drama is like judging life: in Shakespeare's dramas, the aim was to bring back to mind life in its universal meaning, but above all to show us that part of it, through that unique and incomparable perspective, that without Shakespeare we could never have seen. The irreducible fate of the most famous and celebrated Danish prince in history: Hamlet, as well as the soliloquy to be or not to be (Act III scene I), is not greater than life, but the attempt to represent its greatness.

Shakespeare produced Hamlet as a contribution of Art to Nature. As an infinite ego with great and inexhaustible moral responsibility, the idea of Western man has countless illustrious precedents: Homer, Plato and Aristotle, Sophocles and the Bible, Saint Augustine and Dante - just to name a few. But Harold Bloom, one of the most influential American critics, argues that Shakespeare's greatness lies in creating the personality as we modern people understand it. Even more than the other Shakespearean prodigies - Rosalinda, Shylock, Iago, King Lear, Macbeth, Cleopatra, Falstaff - Hamlet is to be understood then, in terms of the American critic, the invention of the human, the inauguration of the personality of modern man.

For Hamlet, the Ego is an abyss, understood as chaos in the depths of total darkness. If Oedipus is the great myth of classicism, Hamlet - along with a few others - is, without doubt, the myth of modernity. Hamlet is modern in the true sense of the word. He is a man in constant search of an ideological, philosophical, and existential awareness. In England, the seventeenth century saw the clash between a medieval world and a mercantile-bourgeois world, God's certainty, and the ascent towards a universe to be re-explanated. Hamlet finds himself in the middle of this clash and decides to escape by refusing the central position, that is, that of the protagonist. In this case, he expresses not the rejection of others' tragedy, but that of each one. Against his own will, Hamlet will be the great protagonist of his very personal tragic event.

For Hamlet, the problem of Being is an inexplicable dream, a privilege for no one. No individual can achieve this ontological status. Therefore, Hamlet is a nostalgic of Being, and "is" only when he wears the mask of madness. But it is a fake madness, just as every actor's mask with which he plays a dramatic fiction is fake. Hamlet is forced to live all the contradictions of his era: wearing the mask of one who has a mad and schizophrenic power, he pretends to be mad without being mad, then he pretends to be in love with Ophelia, leading her to madness and death, and all that has never been comes out through an act of return, due and just: in love only after losing her, he becomes aware of his own madness.

Romantic criticism has defined Hamlet as a tragedy of thought: the protagonist's great rationality has made him reluctant to act. Kierkegaard and Nietzsche were concerned about Hamlet's religious and Dionysian aspects, respectively, while the psychoanalysts reread the work starting from the Oedipus complex. Using the tools of the philosophy of language, it has been analyzed from the perspective of dialectics and semantic structure, while in the last fifty years, it has been plunged into a variety of critical approaches ranging from structuralism to semiotics, from neo-historicism to the feminist movement.

Hamlet is the modern man always looking for a reason, a purpose. A sense that will eventually find its foundation in fiction, just as Shakespeare man found it in the theater. Or in death, with the only regret of leaving passions and big dreams alive. Then the Being, as unattainable, becomes fiction, madness and death.

The rest is silence.

LIST OF CHARACTERS

HAMLET: Protagonist of the tragedy and Prince of Denmark. He is the son of Queen Gertrude and the late King Hamlet and nephew of the present King Claudius, his uncle.

CLAUDIUS: Current king of Denmark, Hamlet's uncle, and his antagonist in the tragedy.

GERTRUDE: Queen of Denmark and mother of Hamlet, now married to Claudius.

POLONIUS: Chamberlain of Elsinore, father of Laertes and Ophelia.

HORATIO: Friend of Hamlet, fellow student at the University of Wittenberg.

OPHELIA: Daughter of Polonius, in love with Hamlet.

LAERTES: Son of Polonius and brother of Ophelia.

FORTINBRAS: Young Prince of Norway, whose father was killed by Hamlet's father.

THE GHOST: The ghost of Hamlet›s father, who claims to have been murdered by Claudius and who invites Hamlet to avenge him. However, it is never certain that the ghost is the dead father: Hamlet speculates that the ghost could be the devil himself, who wants to deceive him and make him commit a murder. The question of who the ghost is and where he comes from is never solved and revealed.

ROSENCRANTZ AND GUILDENSTERN: Two courtiers, former friends of Hamlet.

OSRIC: a courtier.

VOLTEMAND AND CORNELIUS: Courtiers who are sent to Norway to convince Fortinbras not to attack Denmark.

MARCELLUS AND BARNARDO: two guards.

REYNALDO: Servant of Polonius.

ᴀCT 1

Scene 1

Two guards at E astle see the ghost of the recently dead King Hamlet. Horatio decides to tell Hamlet.

*Enter **BARNARDO** and **FRANCISCO**, two sentinels*

BARNARDO
Who's there?!

FRANCISCO
Nay, answer me: stand, and unfold yourself.

BARNARDO
Long live the king!

FRANCISCO
Bernardo?

BARNARDO
He.

FRANCISCO

WBARNARDO
'Tis now struck twelve; get thee to bed, Francisco.

FRANCISCO
For this relief much thanks: 'tis bitter cold, And I am sick at heart.

BARNARDO
Have you had quiet guard?

FRANCISCO
Not a mouse stirring.

BARNARDO
Well, good night.
If you do meet Horatio and Marcellus,
The rivals of my watch, bid them make haste.

FRANCISCO
I think I hear them. Stand, ho! Who's there?

*Enter **HORATIO** and **MARCELLUS***

HORATIO
Friends to this ground.

MARCELLUS
And liegemen to the Dane.

FRANCISCO
Give you good night.

MARCELLUS
O, farewell, honest soldier. Who hath relieved you?

FRANCISCO
Barnardo has my place. Give you good night.

*Exit **FRANCISCO***

MARCELLUS
Holla, Barnardo

BARNARDO
Say what, is Horatio there?

HORATIO
A piece of him.

BARNARDO
Welcome, Horatio.—Welcome, good Marcellus.

MARCELLUS
What, has this thing appeared again tonight?

BARNARDO
I have seen nothing.

MARCELLUS
Horatio says 'tis but our fantasy
And will not let belief take hold of him
Touching this dreaded sight twice seen of us.
Therefore I have entreated him along
With us to watch the minutes of this night,
That if again this apparition come
He may approve our eyes and speak to it.

HORATIO
Tush, tush, 'twill not appear.

BARNARDO
Sit down a while
And let us once again assail your ears,
That are so fortified against our story,
What we have two nights seen.

HORATIO
Well, sit we down,
And let us hear Barnardo speak of this.

BARNARDO
Last night of all,
When yond same star that's westward from the pole
Had made his course t' illume that part of heaven
Where now it burns, Marcellus and myself,
The bell then beating one—

Enter **GHOST**

MARCELLUS
Peace, break thee off. Look where it comes again!

BARNARDO
In the same figure like the king that's dead.

MARCELLUS
*(to **HORATIO**)* Thou art a scholar. Speak to it, Horatio.

BARNARDO
Looks it not like the king? Mark it, Horatio.

HORATIO
Most like. It harrows me with fear and wonder.

BARNARDO
It would be spoke to.

MARCELLUS
Question it, Horatio.

HORATIO

What art thou that usurp'st this time of night
Together with that fair and warlike form
In which the majesty of buried Denmark
Did sometimes march? By heaven, I charge thee, speak.

MARCELLUS

It is offended.

BARNARDO

See, it stalks away.

HORATIO

Stay! Speak, speak! I charge thee, speak!

Exit **GHOST**

MARCELLUS

'Tis gone and will not answer.

BARNARDO

How now, Horatio? You tremble and look pale.
Is not this something more than fantasy?
What think you on 't?

HORATIO

Before my God, I might not this believe
Without the sensible and true avouch
Of mine own eyes.

MARCELLUS

Is it not like the king?

HORATIO

As thou art to thyself.
Such was the very armour he had on
When he the ambitious Norway combated.
So frowned he once when, in an angry parle,
He smote the sledded Polacks on the ice.
'Tis strange.

MARCELLUS

Thus twice before, and jump at this dead hour,
With martial stalk hath he gone by our watch.

HORATIO

In what particular thought to work I know not,
But in the gross and scope of mine opinion
This bodes some strange eruption to our state.

MARCELLUS

Good now, sit down and tell me, he that knows,
Why this same strict and most observant watch
So nightly toils the subject of the land,
And why such daily cast of brazen cannon
And foreign mart for implements of war,
Why such impress of shipwrights, whose sore task
Does not divide the Sunday from the week.
What might be toward, that this sweaty haste
Doth make the night joint laborer with the day?
Who is 't that can inform me?

HORATIO

That can I.
At least, the whisper goes so: our last king,
Whose image even but now appeared to us,
Was, as you know, by Fortinbras of Norway,
Thereto pricked on by a most emulate pride,

Dared to the combat; in which our valiant Hamlet
(For so this side of our known world esteemed him)
Did slay this Fortinbras, who by a sealed compact
Well ratified by law and heraldry,
Did forfeit, with his life, all those his lands
Which he stood seized of to the conqueror,
Against the which a moiety competent
Was gagèd by our king, which had returned
To the inheritance of Fortinbras
Had he been vanquisher, as, by the same covenant
And carriage of the article designed,
His fell to Hamlet. Now, sir, young Fortinbras,
Of unimprovèd mettle hot and full,
Hath in the skirts of Norway here and there
Sharked up a list of lawless resolutes,
For food and diet, to some enterprise
That hath a stomach in 't, which is no other—
As it doth well appear unto our state—
But to recover of us, by strong hand
And terms compulsatory, those foresaid lands
So by his father lost. And this, I take it,
Is the main motive of our preparations,
The source of this our watch, and the chief head
Of this posthaste and rummage in the land.

BARNARDO
I think it be no other but e'en so.
Well may it sort that this portentous figure
Comes armèd through our watch so like the king
That was and is the question of these wars.

HORATIO
A mote it is to trouble the mind's eye.
In the most high and palmy state of Rome,

A little ere the mightiest Julius fell,
The graves stood tenantless and the sheeted dead
Did squeak and gibber in the Roman streets
As stars with trains of fire and dews of blood,
Disasters in the sun, and the moist star
Upon whose influence Neptune's empire stands
Was sick almost to doomsday with eclipse.
And even the like precurse of feared events,
As harbingers preceding still the fates
And prologue to the omen coming on,
Have heaven and earth together demonstrated
Unto our climatures and countrymen.

Enter **GHOST**

But soft, behold! Lo, where it comes again.
I'll cross it though it blast me.—Stay, illusion!

GHOST *spreads his arms*

Horatio. But, soft, behold! lo, where it comes again!
I'll cross it, though it blast me.—Stay, illusion! *Act 1. Scene 1.*

If thou hast any sound or use of voice,
Speak to me.
If there be any good thing to be done
That may to thee do ease and grace to me,
Speak to me.
If thou art privy to thy country's fate,
Which happily foreknowing may avoid,
Oh, speak!
Or if thou hast uphoarded in thy life
Extorted treasure in the womb of earth,
For which, they say, you spirits oft walk in death,
Speak of it. Stay and speak!

9

The cock crows

—Stop it, Marcellus.

MARCELLUS
Shall I strike at it with my partisan?

HORATIO
Do, if it will not stand.

BARNARDO
'Tis here.

HORATIO
'Tis here.

Exit **GHOST**

MARCELLUS
'Tis gone.
We do it wrong, being so majestical,
To offer it the show of violence,
For it is, as the air, invulnerable,
And our vain blows malicious mockery.

BARNARDO
It was about to speak when the cock crew.

HORATIO
And then it started like a guilty thing
Upon a fearful summons. I have heard
The cock, that is the trumpet to the morn,
Doth with his lofty and shrill-sounding throat
Awake the god of day, and, at his warning,

Whether in sea or fire, in earth or air,
Th' extravagant and erring spirit hies
To his confine, and of the truth herein
This present object made probation.

MARCELLUS

It faded on the crowing of the cock.
Some say that ever 'gainst that season comes
Wherein our Saviour's birth is celebrated,
The bird of dawning singeth all night long.
160And then, they say, no spirit dare stir abroad.
The nights are wholesome. Then no planets strike,
No fairy takes, nor witch hath power to charm,
So hallowed and so gracious is that time.

HORATIO

So have I heard and do in part believe it.
But look, the morn, in russet mantle clad,
Walks o'er the dew of yon high eastward hill.
Break we our watch up, and by my advice,
Let us impart what we have seen tonight
Unto young Hamlet, for, upon my life,
This spirit, dumb to us, will speak to him.
Do you consent we shall acquaint him with it,
As needful in our loves, fitting our duty?

MARCELLUS

Let's do 't, I pray, and I this morning know
Where we shall find him most conveniently.

Exeunt

ACT 1

Scene 2

Gertrude and King Claudius, who are recently married, ask Hamlet to stay in Denmark a while longer. Horatio tells Hamlet about the ghost.

*Enter **CLAUDIUS**, king of Denmark; **GERTRUDE** the queen;*
***HAMLET**; **POLONIUS**; his son **LAERTES**; and his daughter*
***OPHELIA**; **LORDS** attendant*

CLAUDIUS
Though yet of Hamlet our dear brother's death
The memory be green, and that it us befitted
To bear our hearts in grief and our whole kingdom
To be contracted in one brow of woe,
Yet so far hath discretion fought with nature
That we with wisest sorrow think on him
Together with remembrance of ourselves.
Therefore our sometime sister, now our queen,
Th' imperial jointress to this warlike state,
Have we—as 'twere with a defeated joy,
With an auspicious and a dropping eye,
With mirth in funeral and with dirge in marriage,
In equal scale weighing delight and dole—
Taken to wife. Nor have we herein barred
Your better wisdoms, which have freely gone
With this affair along. For all, our thanks.

Now follows that you know. Young Fortinbras,
Holding a weak supposal of our worth
Or thinking by our late dear brother's death
Our state to be disjoint and out of frame,
Colleaguèd with the dream of his advantage,
He hath not failed to pester us with message
Importing the surrender of those lands
Lost by his father, with all bonds of law,
To our most valiant brother. So much for him.

Enter **VOLTEMAND** *and* **CORNELIUS**

Now for ourself and for this time of meeting
Thus much the business is: we have here writ
To Norway, uncle of young Fortinbras—
Who, impotent and bedrid, scarcely hears
Of this his nephew's purpose—to suppress
His further gait herein, in that the levies,
The lists, and full proportions are all made
Out of his subject; and we here dispatch
You, good Cornelius, and you, Voltemand,
For bearers of this greeting to old Norway,
Giving to you no further personal power
To business with the king more than the scope
Of these dilated articles allow. *(gives them a paper)*
Farewell, and let your haste commend your duty.

CORNELIUS, VOLTEMAND
In that and all things will we show our duty.

CLAUDIUS
We doubt it nothing. Heartily farewell.

Exeunt VOLTEMAND and CORNELIUS

And now, Laertes, what's the news with you?
You told us of some suit. What is 't, Laertes?
You cannot speak of reason to the Dane
And lose your voice. What wouldst thou beg, Laertes,
That shall not be my offer, not thy asking?
The head is not more native to the heart,
The hand more instrumental to the mouth,
Than is the throne of Denmark to thy father.
What wouldst thou have, Laertes?

LAERTES
My dread lord,
Your leave and favor to return to France,
From whence though willingly I came to Denmark
To show my duty in your coronation,
Yet now, I must confess, that duty done,
My thoughts and wishes bend again toward France
And bow them to your gracious leave and pardon.

CLAUDIUS
Have you your father's leave? What says Polonius?

POLONIUS
He hath, my lord, wrung from me my slow leave
By laborsome petition, and at last
Upon his will I sealed my hard consent.
I do beseech you, give him leave to go.

CLAUDIUS
Take thy fair hour, Laertes. Time be thine,
And thy best graces spend it at thy will.—
But now, my cousin Hamlet, and my son—

HAMLET

(aside) A little more than kin and less than kind.

CLAUDIUS

How is it that the clouds still hang on you?

HAMLET

Not so, my lord. I am too much i' the sun.

GERTRUDE

Good Hamlet, cast thy nighted color off,
And let thine eye look like a friend on Denmark.
Do not forever with thy vailèd lids
Seek for thy noble father in the dust.
Thou know'st 'tis common. All that lives must die,
Passing through nature to eternity.

HAMLET

Ay, madam, it is common.

GERTRUDE

If it be, why seems it so particular with thee?

King. How is it that the clouds still hang on you?
Hamlet. Not so, my lord; I am too much i' the sun.
Act I. Scene II.

HAMLET

"Seems," madam? Nay, it is. I know not "seems."
'Tis not alone my inky cloak, good mother,
Nor customary suits of solemn black,
Nor windy suspiration of forced breath,
No, nor the fruitful river in the eye,
Nor the dejected 'havior of the visage,
Together with all forms, moods, shapes of grief,
That can denote me truly. These indeed "seem,"
For they are actions that a man might play.
But I have that within which passeth show,
These but the trappings and the suits of woe.

17

CLAUDIUS

'Tis sweet and commendable in your nature, Hamlet,
To give these mourning duties to your father.
But you must know your father lost a father,
That father lost, lost his, and the survivor bound
In filial obligation for some term
To do obsequious sorrow. But to persever
In obstinate condolement is a course
Of impious stubbornness. 'Tis unmanly grief.
It shows a will most incorrect to heaven,
A heart unfortified, a mind impatient,
An understanding simple and unschooled.
For what we know must be and is as common
As any the most vulgar thing to sense,
Why should we in our peevish opposition
Take it to heart? Fie! 'Tis a fault to heaven,
A fault against the dead, a fault to nature,
To reason most absurd, whose common theme
Is death of fathers, and who still hath cried,
From the first corse till he that died today,
"This must be so." We pray you, throw to earth
This unprevailing woe, and think of us
As of a father. For let the world take note,
You are the most immediate to our throne,
And with no less nobility of love
Than that which dearest father bears his son
Do I impart toward you. For your intent
In going back to school in Wittenberg,
It is most retrograde to our desire.
And we beseech you, bend you to remain
Here in the cheer and comfort of our eye,
Our chiefest courtier, cousin, and our son.

GERTRUDE

Let not thy mother lose her prayers, Hamle

I pray thee, stay with us. Go not to Witter

HAMLET

I shall in all my best obey you, madam.

CLAUDIUS

Why, 'tis a loving and a fair reply.

Be as ourself in Denmark.—Madam, come.

This gentle and unforced accord of Hamlet

Sits smiling to my heart, in grace whereof

No jocund health that Denmark drinks today

But the great cannon to the clouds shall tell,

And the king's rouse the heavens shall bruit again,

Respeaking earthly thunder. Come away.

Flourish. Exeunt all but **HAMLET**

HAMLET

Oh, that this too, too sullied flesh would melt,

Thaw, and resolve itself into a dew,

Or that the Everlasting had not fixed

His canon 'gainst self-slaughter! O God, God!

How weary, stale, flat, and unprofitable

Seem to me all the uses of this world!

Fie on 't, ah fie! 'Tis an unweeded garden

That grows to seed. Things rank and gross in nature

Possess it merely. That it should come to this.

But two months dead—nay, not so much, not two.

So excellent a king, that was to this

Hyperion to a satyr. So loving to my mother

That he might not beteem the winds of heaven

19

Visit her face too roughly.—Heaven and earth,
Must I remember? Why, she would hang on him
As if increase of appetite had grown
By what it fed on, and yet, within a month—
Let me not think on 't. Frailty, thy name is woman!—
A little month, or ere those shoes were old
With which she followed my poor father's body,
Like Niobe, all tears. Why she, even she—
O God, a beast that wants discourse of reason
Would have mourned longer!—married with my uncle,
My father's brother, but no more like my father
Than I to Hercules. Within a month,
Ere yet the salt of most unrighteous tears
Had left the flushing in her gallèd eyes,
She married. O most wicked speed, to post
With such dexterity to incestuous sheets!
It is not nor it cannot come to good,
But break, my heart, for I must hold my tongue.

*Enter **HORATIO, MARCELLUS,** and **BARNARDO***

HORATIO
Hail to your lordship.

HAMLET
I am glad to see you well.—
Horatio? Or I do forget myself?

HORATIO
The same, my lord, and your poor servant ever.

HAMLET
Sir, my good friend, I'll change that name with you.
And what make you from Wittenberg, Horatio?—

Marcellus!

MARCELLUS
My good lord.

HAMLET
(to MARCELLUS*)* I am very glad to see you.—*(to* BARNARDO*)*
Good even, sir.
(to HORATIO*)* —But what, in faith, make you from Wittenberg?

HORATIO
A truant disposition, good my lord.

HAMLET
I would not hear your enemy say so,
Nor shall you do mine ear that violence,
To make it truster of your own report
Against yourself. I know you are no truant.
But what is your affair in Elsinore?
We'll teach you to drink deep ere you depart.

HORATIO
My lord, I came to see your father's funeral.

HAMLET
I pray thee, do not mock me, fellow student.
I think it was to see my mother's wedding.

HORATIO
Indeed, my lord, it followed hard upon.

HAMLET
Thrift, thrift, Horatio! The funeral baked meats
Did coldly furnish forth the marriage tables.
Would I had met my dearest foe in heaven
Or ever I had seen that day, Horatio.
My father—methinks I see my father.

HORATIO
Where, my lord?

HAMLET
In my mind's eye, Horatio.

HORATIO
I saw him once. He was a goodly king.

HAMLET
He was a man. Take him for all in all.
I shall not look upon his like again.

HORATIO
My lord, I think I saw him yesternight.

HAMLET
Saw who?

HORATIO
My lord, the king your father.

HAMLET
The king my father?!

HORATIO
Season your admiration for a while
With an attent ear, till I may deliver,
Upon the witness of these gentlemen,
This marvel to you.

HAMLET
For God's love, let me hear.

HORATIO
Two nights together had these gentlemen,

Marcellus and Barnardo, on their watch,
In the dead waste and middle of the night,
Been thus encountered: a figure like your father,
Armed at point exactly, cap-à-pie,
Appears before them and with solemn march
Goes slow and stately by them. Thrice he walked
By their oppressed and fear-surprisèd eyes
Within his truncheon's length, whilst they, distilled
Almost to jelly with the act of fear,
Stand dumb and speak not to him. This to me
In dreadful secrecy impart they did,
And I with them the third night kept the watch,
Where—as they had delivered, both in time,
Form of the thing, each word made true and good—
The apparition comes. I knew your father.
These hands are not more like.

HAMLET
But where was this?

MARCELLUS
My lord, upon the platform where we watch.

HAMLET
Did you not speak to it?

HORATIO
My lord, I did,
But answer made it none. Yet once methought
It lifted up its head and did address
Itself to motion, like as it would speak.
But even then the morning cock crew loud,
And at the sound it shrunk in haste away
And vanished from our sight.

HAMLET

'Tis very strange.

HORATIO

As I do live, my honored lord, 'tis true.
And we did think it writ down in our duty
To let you know of it.

HAMLET

Indeed, indeed, sirs, but this troubles me.
Hold you the watch tonight?

MARCELLUS, BARNARDO

We do, my lord.

HAMLET

Armed, say you?

MARCELLUS, BARNARDO

Armed, my lord.

HAMLET

From top to toe?

MARCELLUS, BARNARDO

My lord, from head to foot.

HAMLET

Then saw you not his face?

HORATIO

Oh yes, my lord. He wore his beaver up.

HAMLET

What, looked he frowningly?

HORATIO
A countenance more
In sorrow than in anger.

HAMLET
Pale or red?

HORATIO
Nay, very pale.

HAMLET
And fixed his eyes upon you?

HORATIO
Most constantly.

HAMLET
I would I had been there.

HORATIO
It would have much amazed you.

HAMLET
Very like. Stayed it long?

HORATIO
While one with moderate haste might tell a hundred.

MARCELLUS, BARNARDO
Longer, longer.

HORATIO
Not when I saw 't.

HAMLET
His beard was grizzled, no?

HORATIO
It was, as I have seen it in his life,
A sable silvered.

HAMLET
I will watch tonight. Perchance
'Twill walk again.

HORATIO
I warrant it will.

HAMLET
If it assume my noble father's person,
I'll speak to it, though Hell itself should gape
And bid me hold my peace. I pray you all,
If you have hitherto concealed this sight,
Let it be tenable in your silence still.
And whatsoever else shall hap tonight,
Give it an understanding, but no tongue.
I will requite your loves. So fare you well.
Upon the platform, 'twixt eleven and twelve,
I'll visit you.

HORATIO, MARCELLUS, BARNARDO
Our duty to your honor.

HAMLET
ves, as mine to you. Farewell.
Exeunt all but **HAMLET**
My father's spirit in arms. All is not well.
I doubt some foul play. Would the night were come!
Till then sit still, my soul. Foul deeds will rise,
Though all the earth o'erwhelm them, to men's eyes.

Exit

26

ACT 1

Scene 3

Laertes counsels his sister Ophelia not to fall in love with Hamlet, and their father Polonius agrees. Polonius advises Laertes on how to conduct himself at school.

*Enter **LAERTES** and **OPHELIA**, his sister*

LAERTES
My necessaries are embarked. Farewell.
And, sister, as the winds give benefit
And convey is assistant, do not sleep,
But let me hear from you.

OPHELIA
Do you doubt that?

LAERTES
For Hamlet and the trifling of his favor,
Hold it a fashion and a toy in blood,
A violet in the youth of primy nature,
Forward, not permanent, sweet, not lasting,
The perfume and suppliance of a minute.
No more.

OPHELIA
No more but so?

LAERTES

Think it no more.
For nature, crescent, does not grow alone
In thews and bulk, but, as this temple waxes,
The inward service of the mind and soul
Grows wide withal. Perhaps he loves you now,
And now no soil nor cautel doth besmirch
The virtue of his will, but you must fear.
His greatness weighed, his will is not his own,
For he himself is subject to his birth.
He may not, as unvalued persons do,
Carve for himself, for on his choice depends
The safety and health of this whole state.
And therefore must his choice be circumscribed
Unto the voice and yielding of that body
Whereof he is the head. Then if he says he loves you,
It fits your wisdom so far to believe it
As he in his particular act and place
May give his saying deed, which is no further
Than the main voice of Denmark goes withal.
Then weigh what loss your honor may sustain
If with too credent ear you list his songs,
Or lose your heart, or your chaste treasure open
To his unmastered importunity.
Fear it, Ophelia. Fear it, my dear sister,
And keep you in the rear of your affection,
Out of the shot and danger of desire.
The chariest maid is prodigal enough
If she unmask her beauty to the moon.
Virtue itself 'scapes not calumnious strokes.
The canker galls the infants of the spring
Too oft before their buttons be disclosed.
And in the morn and liquid dew of youth,
Contagious blastments are most imminent.

Be wary, then. Best safety lies in fear.
Youth to itself rebels, though none else near.

OPHELIA
I shall the effect of this good lesson keep
As watchman to my heart. But, good my brother,
Do not, as some ungracious pastors do,
Show me the steep and thorny way to heaven
Whiles, like a puffed and reckless libertine,
Himself the primrose path of dalliance treads
And recks not his own rede.

LAERTES
O, fear me not.

Enter **POLONIUS**

I stay too long. But here my father comes.
A double blessing is a double grace.
Occasion smiles upon a second leave.

POLONIUS
Yet here, Laertes? Aboard, aboard, for shame!
The wind sits in the shoulder of your sail
And you are stayed for. There, my blessing with thee.
And these few precepts in thy memory
Look thou character. Give thy thoughts no tongue,
Nor any unproportioned thought his act.
Be thou familiar but by no means vulgar.
Those friends thou hast, and their adoption tried,
Grapple them unto thy soul with hoops of steel,
But do not dull thy palm with entertainment
Of each new-hatched, unfledged comrade. Beware
Of entrance to a quarrel, but being in,

Bear 't that th' opposèd may beware of thee.
Give every man thy ear but few thy voice.
Take each man's censure but reserve thy judgment.
Costly thy habit as thy purse can buy,
But not expressed in fancy—rich, not gaudy,
For the apparel oft proclaims the man,
And they in France of the best rank and station
Are of a most select and generous chief in that.
Neither a borrower nor a lender be,
For loan oft loses both itself and friend,
And borrowing dulls the edge of husbandry.
This above all: to thine own self be true,
And it must follow, as the night the day,
Thou canst not then be false to any man.
Farewell. My blessing season this in thee.

LAERTES
Most humbly do I take my leave, my lord.

POLONIUS
The time invites you. Go. Your servants tend.

LAERTES
Farewell, Ophelia, and remember well
What I have said to you.

OPHELIA
'Tis in my memory locked,
And you yourself shall keep the key of it.

LAERTES
Farewell.

*Exit **LAERTES***

POLONIUS
What is 't, Ophelia, he hath said to you?

OPHELIA
So please you, something touching the Lord Ham.

Polonius. What is 't, Ophelia, he hath said to you?
Ophelia. So please you, something touching the Lord Hamlet.
Act I. Scene III.

POLONIUS
Marry, well bethought.
'Tis told me he hath very oft of late
Given private time to you, and you yourself
Have of your audience been most free and bounteous.
If it be so as so 'tis put on me—
And that in way of caution—I must tell you,
You do not understand yourself so clearly
As it behooves my daughter and your honor.
What is between you? Give me up the truth.

31

OPHELIA

He hath, my lord, of late made many tenders
Of his affection to me.

POLONIUS

Affection! Pooh, you speak like a green girl,
Unsifted in such perilous circumstance.
Do you believe his "tenders," as you call them?

OPHELIA

I do not know, my lord, what I should think.

POLONIUS

Marry, I'll teach you. Think yourself a baby
That you have ta'en these tenders for true pay,
Which are not sterling. Tender yourself more dearly,
Or—not to crack the wind of the poor phrase,
Running it thus—you'll tender me a fool.

OPHELIA

My lord, he hath importuned me with love
In honorable fashion.

POLONIUS

Ay, "fashion" you may call it. Go to, go to.

OPHELIA

And hath given countenance to his speech, my lord,
With almost all the holy vows of heaven.

POLONIUS

Ay, springes to catch woodcocks. I do know,
When the blood burns, how prodigal the soul
Lends the tongue vows. These blazes, daughter,
Giving more light than heat, extinct in both

Even in their promise as it is a-making,
You must not take for fire. From this time
Be somewhat scanter of your maiden presence.
Set your entreatments at a higher rate
Than a command to parley. For Lord Hamlet,
Believe so much in him that he is young,
And with a larger tether may he walk
Than may be given you. In few, Ophelia,
Do not believe his vows, for they are brokers
Not of that dye which their investments show,
But mere implorators of unholy suits,
Breathing like sanctified and pious bawds,
The better to beguile. This is for all:
I would not, in plain terms, from this time forth,
Have you so slander any moment leisure,
As to give words or talk with the Lord Hamlet.
Look to 't, I charge you. Come your ways.

OPHELIA
I shall obey, my lord.

Exeunt

ACT 1

Scene 4

Hamlet waits with Horatio and Marcellus for the ghost to appear. When it does appear, Hamlet runs after it, and the others follow.

*Enter **HAMLET**, **HORATIO**, and **MARCELLUS***

HAMLET
The air bites shrewdly. It is very cold.

HORATIO
It is a nipping and an eager air.

HAMLET
What hour now?

HORATIO
I think it lacks of twelve.

MARCELLUS
No, it is struck.

HORATIO
Indeed? I heard it not. It then draws near the season
Wherein the spirit held his wont to walk.
A flourish of trumpets and two pieces of ordnance goes off
What does this mean, my lord?

HAMLET

The king doth wake tonight and takes his rouse,
Keeps wassail and the swaggering upspring reels,
And, as he drains his draughts of Rhenish down,
The kettle-drum and trumpet thus bray out
The triumph of his pledge.

HORATIO

Is it a custom?

HAMLET

Ay, marry, is 't.
But to my mind, though I am native here
And to the manner born, it is a custom
More honored in the breach than the observance.
This heavy-headed revel east and west
Makes us traduced and taxed of other nations.
They clepe us drunkards and with swinish phrase
Soil our addition. And indeed it takes
From our achievements, though performed at height,
The pith and marrow of our attribute.
So oft it chances in particular men
That for some vicious mole of nature in them—
As in their birth (wherein they are not guilty,
Since nature cannot choose his origin),
By the o'ergrowth of some complexion,
Oft breaking down the pales and forts of reason,
Or by some habit that too much o'erleavens
The form of plausive manners—that these men,
Carrying, I say, the stamp of one defect,
Being nature's livery or fortune's star,
Their virtues else (be they as pure as grace,
As infinite as man may undergo)
Shall in the general censure take corruption

From that particular fault. The dram of evil
Doth all the noble substance of a doubt
To his own scandal.

Enter **GHOST**

HORATIO
Look, my lord, it comes!

HAMLET
Angels and ministers of grace defend us!
Be thou a spirit of health or goblin damned,
Bring with thee airs from heaven or blasts from hell,
Be thy intents wicked or charitable,
Thou comest in such a questionable shape
That I will speak to thee. I'll call thee "Hamlet,"
"King," "Father," "royal Dane." O, answer me!
Let me not burst in ignorance, but tell
Why thy canonized bones, hearsed in death,
Have burst their cerements; why the sepulcher,
Wherein we saw thee quietly interred,
Hath oped his ponderous and marble jaws
To cast thee up again. What may this mean,
That thou, dead corse, again in complete steel
Revisits thus the glimpses of the moon,
Making night hideous and we fools of nature,
So horridly to shake our disposition
With thoughts beyond the reaches of our souls?
Say why is this? Wherefore? What should we do?

37

GHOST *beckons* **HAMLET**

HORATIO

It beckons you to go away with it,
As if it some impartment did desire
To you alone.

MARCELLUS

Look, with what courteous action
It waves you to a more removèd ground.
But do not go with it.

HORATIO

No, by no means.

HAMLET
It will not speak. Then I will follow it.

HORATIO
Do not, my lord.

HAMLET
Why, what should be the fear?
I do not set my life in a pin's fee,
And for my soul—what can it do to that,
Being a thing immortal as itself?
It waves me forth again. I'll follow it.

HORATIO
What if it tempt you toward the flood, my lord,
Or to the dreadful summit of the cliff
That beetles o'er his base into the sea,
And there assume some other horrible form,
Which might deprive your sovereignty of reason
And draw you into madness? Think of it.
The very place puts toys of desperation,
Without more motive, into every brain
That looks so many fathoms to the sea
And hears it roar beneath.

HAMLET
It waves me still.
—Go on. I'll follow thee.

MARCELLUS
You shall not go, my lord.

MARCELLUS and HORATIO try to hold HAMLET back

HAMLET
Hold off your hands.

HORATIO
Be ruled. You shall not go.

HAMLET
My fate cries out
And makes each petty artery in this body
As hardy as the Nemean lion's nerve.
Still am I called.—Unhand me, gentlemen.
(draws his sword)
By heaven, I'll make a ghost of him that lets me.
I say, away!—Go on. I'll follow thee.

*Exeunt **GHOST** and **HAMLET***

HORATIO
He waxes desperate with imagination.

MARCELLUS
Let's follow. 'Tis not fit thus to obey him.

HORATIO
Have after. To what issue will this come?

MARCELLUS
Something is rotten in the state of Denmark.

HORATIO
Heaven will direct it.

MARCELLUS
Nay, let's follow him.

Exeunt

ACT 1

Scene 5

The ghost of Hamlet's father says that Claudius murdered him with poison, and that he wants Hamlet to kill Claudius, but spare Gertrude. Hamlet swears he will and tells his companions that he will pretend to be insane to get to the truth.

*Enter **GHOST** and **HAMLET***

HAMLET
Where wilt thou lead me? Speak, I'll go no further.

GHOST
Mark me.

HAMLET
I will.

GHOST
My hour is almost come
When I to sulfurous and tormenting flames
Must render up myself.

HAMLET
Alas, poor ghost!

GHOST
Pity me not, but lend thy serious hearing
To what I shall unfold.

HAMLET
Speak. I am bound to hear.

GHOST
So art thou to revenge when thou shalt hear.

HAMLET
What?

GHOST
I am thy father's spirit,
Doomed for a certain term to walk the night
And for the day confined to fast in fires,
Till the foul crimes done in my days of nature
Are burnt and purged away. But that I am forbid
To tell the secrets of my prison house,
I could a tale unfold whose lightest word
Would harrow up thy soul, freeze thy young blood,
Make thy two eyes, like stars, start from their spheres,
Thy knotted and combinèd locks to part
And each particular hair to stand on end,
Like quills upon the fearful porpentine.
But this eternal blazon must not be
To ears of flesh and blood. List, list, O, list!
If thou didst ever thy dear father love—

HAMLET
O God!

GHOST
Revenge his foul and most unnatural murder.

HAMLET
Murder?

GHOST
Murder most foul, as in the best it is.
But this most foul, strange and unnatural.

HAMLET
Haste me to know 't, that I, with wings as swift
As meditation or the thoughts of love,
May sweep to my revenge.

GHOST
I find thee apt,
And duller shouldst thou be than the fat weed
That roots itself in ease on Lethe wharf,
Wouldst thou not stir in this. Now, Hamlet, hear.
'Tis given out that, sleeping in my orchard,
A serpent stung me. So the whole ear of Denmark
Is by a forgèd process of my death
Rankly abused. But know, thou noble youth,
The serpent that did sting thy father's life
Now wears his crown.

HAMLET
O my prophetic soul! My uncle?

GHOST
Ay, that incestuous, that adulterate beast,
With witchcraft of his wit, with traitorous gifts—
O wicked wit and gifts, that have the power
So to seduce!—won to his shameful lust
The will of my most seeming-virtuous queen.
O Hamlet, what a falling off was there!
From me, whose love was of that dignity

That it went hand in hand even with the vow
I made to her in marriage, and to decline
Upon a wretch whose natural gifts were poor
To those of mine.
But virtue, as it never will be moved,
Though lewdness court it in a shape of heaven,
So lust, though to a radiant angel linked,
Will sate itself in a celestial bed
And prey on garbage.
But soft! Methinks I scent the morning air.
Brief let me be. Sleeping within my orchard,
My custom always of the afternoon,
Upon my secure hour thy uncle stole
With juice of cursed hebenon in a vial,
And in the porches of my ears did pour
The leperous distilment, whose effect
Holds such an enmity with blood of man
That swift as quicksilver it courses through
The natural gates and alleys of the body
And with a sudden vigor doth posset
And curd, like eager droppings into milk,
The thin and wholesome blood. So did it mine.
And a most instant tetter barked about,
Most lazar-like, with vile and loathsome crust
All my smooth body.
Thus was I, sleeping, by a brother's hand
Of life, of crown, of queen at once dispatched,
Cut off even in the blossoms of my sin,
Unhouseled, disappointed, unaneled.
No reckoning made, but sent to my account
With all my imperfections on my head.
Oh, horrible, oh, horrible, most horrible!
If thou hast nature in thee, bear it not.
Let not the royal bed of Denmark be

A couch for luxury and damnèd incest.
But howsoever thou pursuest this act,
Taint not thy mind, nor let thy soul contrive
Against thy mother aught. Leave her to heaven
And to those thorns that in her bosom lodge
To prick and sting her. Fare thee well at once.
The glowworm shows the matin to be near,
And 'gins to pale his uneffectual fire.
Adieu, adieu, adieu. Remember me.

Exit

HAMLET
O all you host of heaven! O earth! What else?
And shall I couple hell? Oh, fie! Hold, hold, my heart,
And you, my sinews, grow not instant old,
But bear me stiffly up. Remember thee!
Ay, thou poor ghost, whiles memory holds a seat
In this distracted globe. Remember thee!
Yea, from the table of my memory
I'll wipe away all trivial fond records,
All saws of books, all forms, all pressures past
That youth and observation copied there,
And thy commandment all alone shall live
Within the book and volume of my brain,
Unmixed with baser matter. Yes, by heaven!
O most pernicious woman!
O villain, villain, smiling, damnèd villain!
My tables!—Meet it is I set it down
That one may smile, and smile, and be a villain.
At least I'm sure it may be so in Denmark. *(writes)*
So, uncle, there you are. Now to my word.
It is "Adieu, adieu. Remember me."
I have sworn 't.

*Enter **HORATIO** and **MARCELLUS***

HORATIO
My lord, my lord!

MARCELLUS
Lord Hamlet—

HORATIO
Heaven secure him!

HAMLET
So be it.

HORATIO
Illo, ho, ho, my lord!

HAMLET
Hillo, ho, ho, boy. Come, bird, come.

MARCELLUS
How is 't, my noble lord?

HORATIO
What news, my lord?

HAMLET
Oh, wonderful!

HORATIO
Good my lord, tell it.

HAMLET
No. You'll reveal it.

HORATIO
Not I, my lord, by heaven.

MARCELLUS
Nor I, my lord.

HAMLET
How say you, then? Would heart of man once think it?
But you'll be secret?

HORATIO, MARCELLUS
Ay, by heaven, my lord.

HAMLET
There's ne'er a villain dwelling in all Denmark
But he's an arrant knave.

HORATIO
There needs no ghost, my lord, come from the grave
To tell us this.

HAMLET
Why, right, you are in the right.
And so, without more circumstance at all,
I hold it fit that we shake hands and part.
You, as your business and desire shall point you—
For every man has business and desire,
Such as it is—and for my own poor part,
Look you, I'll go pray.

HORATIO
These are but wild and whirling words, my lord.

HAMLET
I'm sorry they offend you, heartily.
Yes faith, heartily.

HORATIO
There's no offense, my lord.

HAMLET
Yes, by Saint Patrick, but there is, Horatio,
And much offense too. Touching this vision here,
It is an honest ghost, that let me tell you.
For your desire to know what is between us,
O'ermaster 't as you may. And now, good friends,
As you are friends, scholars and soldiers,
Give me one poor request.

HORATIO
What is 't, my lord? We will.

HAMLET
Never make known what you have seen tonight.

HORATIO, MARCELLUS
My lord, we will not.

HAMLET
Nay, but swear 't.

HORATIO
In faith, my lord, not I.

MARCELLUS
Nor I, my lord, in faith.

HAMLET
Upon my sword.

MARCELLUS
We have sworn, my lord, already.

HAMLET
Indeed, upon my sword, indeed.

GHOST

(cries under the stage) Swear!

HAMLET

Ha, ha, boy! Sayst thou so? Art thou there, truepenny?
Come on, you hear this fellow in the cellarage.
Consent to swear.

HORATIO

Propose the oath, my lord.

HAMLET

Never to speak of this that you have seen.
Swear by my sword.

GHOST

(beneath)   Swear.

HAMLET

Hic et ubique? Then we'll shift our ground.
Come hither, gentlemen,
And lay your hands again upon my sword.
Swear by my sword
Never to speak of this that you have heard.

GHOST

(beneath) Swear by his sword.

HAMLET

Well said, old mole! Canst work i' th' earth so fast?
A worthy pioneer! Once more remove, good friends.

HORATIO

O day and night, but this is wondrous strange!

HAMLET

And therefore as a stranger give it welcome.
There are more things in heaven and earth, Horatio,
Than are dreamt of in your philosophy. But come,
Here, as before, never, so help you mercy,
How strange or odd soe'er I bear myself
(As I perchance hereafter shall think meet
To put an antic disposition on),
That you, at such times seeing me, never shall—
With arms encumbered thus, or this headshake,
Or by pronouncing of some doubtful phrase,
As "Well, well, we know," or "We could an if we would,"
Or "If we list to speak," or "There be an if they might,"
Or such ambiguous giving out—to note
That you know aught of me. This not to do,
So grace and mercy at your most need help you,
Swear.

GHOST

(beneath) Swear!

HAMLET

Rest, rest, perturbèd spirit!—So, gentlemen,
With all my love I do commend me to you,
And what so poor a man as Hamlet is
May do, to express his love and friending to you,
God willing, shall not lack. Let us go in together,
And still your fingers on your lips, I pray.
The time is out of joint. O cursèd spite,
That ever I was born to set it right!
Nay, come, let's go together.

Exeunt

ACT 2

Scene 1

Polonius sends money to his son Laertes, and Ophelia tells her father that Hamlet is behaving strangely.

*Enter **POLONIUS** with his man **REYNALDO***

POLONIUS
Give him this money and these notes, Reynaldo.

REYNALDO
I will, my lord.

POLONIUS
You shall do marvelous wisely, good Reynaldo,
Before you visit him, to make inquire
Of his behavior.

REYNALDO
My lord, I did intend it.

POLONIUS
Marry, well said, very well said. Look you, sir,
Inquire me first what Danskers are in Paris,
And how, and who, what means, and where they keep
What company at what expense; and finding
By this encompassment and drift of question

That they do know my son, come you more nearer
Than your particular demands will touch it.
Take you, as 'twere, some distant knowledge of him,
As thus: "I know his father and his friends,
And, in part, him." Do you mark this, Reynaldo?

REYNALDO
Ay, very well, my lord.

POLONIUS
"And in part him, but," you may say, "not well.
But, if 't be he I mean, he's very wild.
Addicted so and so.—" And there put on him
What forgeries you please. Marry, none so rank
As may dishonor him. Take heed of that.
But, sir, such wanton, wild, and usual slips
As are companions noted and most known
To youth and liberty.

REYNALDO
As gaming, my lord?

POLONIUS
Ay, or drinking, fencing, swearing,
Quarreling, drabbing—you may go so far.

REYNALDO
My lord, that would dishonor him!

POLONIUS
'Faith, no, as you may season it in the charge.
You must not put another scandal on him
That he is open to incontinency.
That's not my meaning. But breathe his faults so quaintly
That they may seem the taints of liberty,

The flash and outbreak of a fiery mind,
A savageness in unreclaimèd blood,
Of general assault.

REYNALDO
But, my good lord—

POLONIUS
Wherefore should you do this?

REYNALDO
Ay, my lord. I would know that.

POLONIUS
Marry, sir, here's my drift:
(And I believe it is a fetch of wit)
You, laying these slight sullies on my son
As 'twere a thing a little soiled i' th' working—
Mark you, your party in converse, him you would sound,
Having ever seen in the prenominate crimes
The youth you breathe of guilty, be assured
He closes with you in this consequence:
"Good sir" or so, or "Friend," or "Gentleman,"
According to the phrase or the addition
Of man and country.

REYNALDO
My lord.

POLONIUS
And then, sir, does he this, he does— What was I about to say? By the mass, I was about to say something. Where did I leave?

REYNALDO
At "closes in the consequence," at "'friend,'
Or so" and "gentleman.'"

53

POLONIUS
At "closes in the consequence." Ay, marry.
He closes thus: "I know the gentleman.
I saw him yesterday"—or "t' other day,"
Or then, or then, with such or such—"and, as you say,
There was he gaming, there o'ertook in's rouse,
There falling out at tennis," or, perchance,
"I saw him enter such a house of sale"—
Videlicet a brothel, or so forth. See you now,
Your bait of falsehood takes this carp of truth.
And thus do we of wisdom and of reach,
With windlasses and with assays of bias,
By indirections find directions out.
So by my former lecture and advice
Shall you my son. You have me, have you not?

REYNALDO
My lord, I have.

POLONIUS
God be wi' you. Fare you well.

REYNALDO
Good my lord.

POLONIUS
Observe his inclination in yourself.

REYNALDO
I shall, my lord.

POLONIUS
And let him ply his music.

REYNALDO
Well, my lord.

POLONIUS
Farewell.

*Exit **REYNALDO***

*Enter **OPHELIA***

How now, Ophelia? What's the matter?

OPHELIA
O my lord, my lord, I have been so affrighted!

Polonius. How now, Ophelia! what's the matter?
Ophelia. Alas! my lord, I have been so affrighted!   *Act II. Scene I.*

POLONIUS
With what, i' th' name of God?

OPHELIA

My lord, as I was sewing in my closet,
Lord Hamlet, with his doublet all unbraced;
No hat upon his head; his stockings fouled,
Ungartered, and down-gyvèd to his ankle;
Pale as his shirt; his knees knocking each other;
And with a look so piteous in purport
As if he had been loosèd out of hell
To speak of horrors—he comes before me.

POLONIUS

Mad for thy love?

OPHELIA

My lord, I do not know.
But truly, I do fear it.

POLONIUS

What said he?

OPHELIA

He took me by the wrist and held me hard.
Then goes he to the length of all his arm,
And, with his other hand thus o'er his brow,
He falls to such perusal of my face
As he would draw it. Long stayed he so.
At last, a little shaking of mine arm
And thrice his head thus waving up and down,
He raised a sigh so piteous and profound
As it did seem to shatter all his bulk
And end his being. That done, he lets me go,
And, with his head over his shoulder turned,
He seemed to find his way without his eyes,
For out o' doors he went without their helps,
And to the last bended their light on me.

POLONIUS

Come, go with me. I will go seek the king.
This is the very ecstasy of love,
Whose violent property fordoes itself
And leads the will to desperate undertakings
As oft as any passion under heaven
That does afflict our natures. I am sorry.
What, have you given him any hard words of late?

OPHELIA

No, my good lord. But as you did command
I did repel his fetters and denied
His access to me.

POLONIUS

That hath made him mad.
I am sorry that with better heed and judgment
I had not quoted him. I feared he did but trifle
And meant to wreck thee. But beshrew my jealousy!
By heaven, it is as proper to our age
To cast beyond ourselves in our opinions
As it is common for the younger sort
To lack discretion. Come, go we to the king.
This must be known, which, being kept close, might move
More grief to hide than hate to utter love.
Come.

Exeunt

ACT 2

Scene 2

Claudius and Gertrude try to determine the cause of Hamlet's strange behavior, summoning help from two of his old friends, Rosencrantz and Guildenstern. A troupe of actors arrive. Hamlet plans to use the troupe to test Claudius.

*Flourish. Enter King **CLAUDIUS** and Queen **GERTRUDE**, **ROSENCRANTZ** and **GUILDENSTERN**, and attendants*

CLAUDIUS
Welcome, dear Rosencrantz and Guildenstern.
Moreover that we much did long to see you,
The need we have to use you did provoke
Our hasty sending. Something have you heard
Of Hamlet's "transformation"—so call it
Since nor th' exterior nor the inward man
Resembles that it was. What it should be,
More than his father's death, that thus hath put him
So much from th' understanding of himself,
I cannot dream of. I entreat you both
That, being of so young days brought up with him
And since so neighbored to his youth and 'havior,
That you vouchsafe your rest here in our court
Some little time so by your companies
To draw him on to pleasures and to gather,

So much as from occasion you may glean,
Whether aught, to us unknown, afflicts him thus
That, opened, lies within our remedy.

GERTRUDE
Good gentlemen, he hath much talked of you.
And sure I am two men there are not living
To whom he more adheres. If it will please you
To show us so much gentry and good will
As to expend your time with us awhile
For the supply and profit of our hope,
Your visitation shall receive such thanks
As fits a king's remembrance.

ROSENCRANTZ
Both your majesties
Might, by the sovereign power you have of us,
Put your dread pleasures more into command
Than to entreaty.

GUILDENSTERN
But we both obey
And here give up ourselves, in the full bent,
To lay our service freely at your feet
To be commanded.

CLAUDIUS
Thanks, Rosencrantz and gentle Guildenstern.

GERTRUDE
Thanks, Guildenstern and gentle Rosencrantz.
And I beseech you instantly to visit
My too much changèd son. Go, some of you,
And bring these gentlemen where Hamlet is.

GUILDENSTERN

Heavens make our presence and our practices
Pleasant and helpful to him!

GERTRUDE

Ay, amen!

*Exeunt **ROSENCRANTZ** and **GUILDENSTERN**, escorted by
attendants*

*Enter **POLONIUS***

POLONIUS

Th' ambassadors from Norway, my good lord,
Are joyfully returned.

CLAUDIUS

Thou still hast been the father of good news.

POLONIUS

Have I, my lord? I assure my good liege,
I hold my duty as I hold my soul,
Both to my God and to my gracious king.
And I do think—or else this brain of mine
Hunts not the trail of policy so sure
As it hath used to do—that I have found
The very cause of Hamlet's lunacy.

CLAUDIUS

Oh, speak of that. That do I long to hear.

POLONIUS

Give first admittance to th' ambassadors.

My news shall be the fruit to that great feast.

CLAUDIUS

Thyself do grace to them, and bring them in.

*Exit **POLONIUS***

He tells me, my dear Gertrude, he hath found

The head and source of all your son's distemper.

GERTRUDE

I doubt it is no other but the main:

His father's death and our o'erhasty marriage.

*Enter **POLONIUS** with ambassadors **VOLTEMAND** and*
CORNELIUS

CLAUDIUS

Well, we shall sift him.—Welcome, my good friends!

Say, Voltemand, what from our brother Norway?

VOLTEMAND

Most fair return of greetings and desires.

Upon our first, he sent out to suppress

His nephew's levies, which to him appeared

To be a preparation 'gainst the Polack,

But, better looked into, he truly found

It was against your highness. Whereat grieved—

That so his sickness, age, and impotence

Was falsely borne in hand—sends out arrests

On Fortinbras, which he, in brief, obeys,

Receives rebuke from Norway, and in fine
Makes vow before his uncle never more
To give th' assay of arms against your majesty.
Whereon old Norway, overcome with joy,
Gives him three thousand crowns in annual fee
And his commission to employ those soldiers,
So levied as before, against the Polack,
With an entreaty, herein further shown,
That it might please you to give quiet pass
Through your dominions for this enterprise,
On such regards of safety and allowance
As therein are set down. *(gives* CLAUDIUS *a document*

CLAUDIUS
It likes us well,
And at our more considered time we'll read,
Answer, and think upon this business.
Meantime we thank you for your well-took labor.
Go to your rest. At night we'll feast together.
Most welcome home!

Exeunt **VOLTEMAND** *and* **CORNELIUS**

POLONIUS
This business is well ended.
My liege and madam, to expostulate
What majesty should be, what duty is,
Why day is day, night night, and time is time,
Were nothing but to waste night, day, and time.
Therefore, since brevity is the soul of wit
And tediousness the limbs and outward flourishes,
I will be brief: your noble son is mad.
Mad call I it, for, to define true madness,

What is 't but to be nothing else but mad?
But let that go.

GERTRUDE
More matter, with less art.

POLONIUS
Madam, I swear I use no art at all.
That he is mad, 'tis true. Tis true, 'tis pity,
And pity 'tis 'tis true—a foolish figure,
But farewell it, for I will use no art.
Mad let us grant him then. And now remains
That we find out the cause of this effect,
Or rather say, the cause of this defect,
For this effect defective comes by cause.
Thus it remains, and the remainder thus. Perpend.
I have a daughter—have while she is mine—
Who in her duty and obedience, mark,
Hath given me this. Now gather and surmise.
(reads a letter) "To the celestial and my soul's idol, the most
beautified Ophelia"—That's an ill phrase, a vile phrase.
"Beautified" is a vile phrase. But you shall hear. Thus: *(reads the
letter)*"In her excellent white bosom, these," etc.—

GERTRUDE
Came this from Hamlet to her?

POLONIUS
Good madam, stay a while. I will be faithful.
(reads the letter)
"Doubt thou the stars are fire,
Doubt that the sun doth move,
Doubt truth to be a liar,
But never doubt I love.
O dear Ophelia, I am ill at these numbers. I have not art to

reckon my groans, but that I love thee best, oh, m
it. Adieu.
Thine evermore, most dear lady,
whilst this machine is to him,
Hamlet."
This in obedience hath my daughter shown me,
And more above, hath his solicitings,
As they fell out by time, by means, and place,
All given to mine ear.

CLAUDIUS
But how hath she received his love?

POLONIUS
What do you think of me?

CLAUDIUS
As of a man faithful and honorable.

POLONIUS
I would fain prove so. But what might you think,
When I had seen this hot love on the wing—
As I perceived it, I must tell you that,
Before my daughter told me—what might you,
Or my dear majesty your queen here, think,
If I had played the desk or table-book,
Or given my heart a winking, mute and dumb,
Or looked upon this love with idle sight?
What might you think? No, I went round to work,
And my young mistress thus I did bespeak:
"Lord Hamlet is a prince out of thy star.
This must not be." And then I prescripts gave her,
That she should lock herself from his resort,
Admit no messengers, receive no tokens.
Which done, she took the fruits of my advice;

And he, repelled—a short tale to make—
Fell into a sadness, then into a fast,
Thence to a watch, thence into a weakness,
Thence to a lightness, and, by this declension,
Into the madness wherein now he raves
And all we mourn for.

CLAUDIUS
(to GERTRUDE *)* Do you think 'tis this?

GERTRUDE
It may be, very like.

POLONIUS
Hath there been such a time—I would fain know that—
That I have positively said, "'Tis so,"
When it proved otherwise?

CLAUDIUS
Not that I know.

POLONIUS
(points to his head and shoulders)
Take this from this if this be otherwise.
If circumstances lead me, I will find
Where truth is hid, though it were hid indeed
Within the center.

CLAUDIUS
How may we try it further?

POLONIUS
You know sometimes he walks four hours together
Here in the lobby.

GERTRUDE
So he does indeed.

POLONIUS
At such a time I'll loose my daughter to him.
(to CLAUDIUS*)* Be you and I behind an arras then,
Mark the encounter. If he love her not
And be not from his reason fall'n thereon,
Let me be no assistant for a state
But keep a farm and carters.

CLAUDIUS
We will try it.

*Enter **HAMLET**, reading on a book*

GERTRUDE
But look where sadly the poor wretch comes reading.

POLONIUS
Away, I do beseech you, both away.
I'll board him presently. O, give me leave.

*Exeunt **CLAUDIUS** and **GERTRUDE***

How does my good Lord Hamlet?

HAMLET
Well, God-'a'-mercy.

POLONIUS
Do you know me, my lord?

HAMLET
Excellent well. You are a fishmonger.

POLONIUS
Not I, my lord.

HAMLET

Then I would you were so honest a man.

POLONIUS

Honest, my lord?

HAMLET

Ay, sir. To be honest, as this world goes, is to be one man picked out of ten thousand.

POLONIUS

That's very true, my lord.

HAMLET

For if the sun breed maggots in a dead dog, being a good kissing carrion— Have you a daughter?

POLONIUS

I have, my lord.

HAMLET

Let her not walk i' th' sun. Conception is a blessing, but, as your daughter may conceive—Friend, look to 't.

POLONIUS

(aside) How say you by that? Still harping on my daughter. Yet he knew me not at first. He said I was a fishmonger. He is far gone, far gone. And truly in my youth I suffered much extremity for love, very near this. I'll speak to him again.—*(to HAMLET)* What do you read, my lord?

HAMLET

Words, words, words.

POLONIUS

What is the matter, my lord?

HAMLET

Between who?

POLONIUS

I mean, the matter that you read, my lord.

HAMLET

Slanders, sir. For the satirical rogue says here that old men have gray beards, that their faces are wrinkled, their eyes purging thick amber and plum-tree gum, and that they have a plentiful lack of wit, together with most weak hams—all which, sir, though I most powerfully and potently believe, yet I hold it not honesty to have it thus set down; for yourself, sir, should be old as I am, if like a crab you could go backward.

POLONIUS

(aside) Though this be madness, yet there is method in 't.—*(to HAMLET)* Will you walk out of the air, my lord?

HAMLET

Into my grave.

POLONIUS

Indeed, that is out of the air. *(aside)* How pregnant sometimes his replies are. A happiness that often madness hits on, which reason and sanity could not so prosperously be delivered of. I will leave him and suddenly contrive the means of meeting between him and my daughter.—*(to HAMLET)* My honorable lord, I will most humbly take my leave of you.

HAMLET

You cannot, sir, take from me any thing that I will more willingly part withal—except my life, except my life, except my life.

POLONIUS

Fare you well, my lord.

HAMLET

(aside) These tedious old fools!

*Enter **ROSENCRANTZ** and **GUILDENSTERN***

POLONIUS

You go to seek the Lord Hamlet. There he is.

ROSENCRANTZ

God save you, sir!

*Exit **POLONIUS***

GUILDENSTERN

My honored lord!

ROSENCRANTZ

My most dear lord!

HAMLET

My excellent good friends! How dost thou, Guildenstern?
Ah, Rosencrantz! Good lads, how do you both?

ROSENCRANTZ

As the indifferent children of the earth.

GUILDENSTERN

Happy, in that we are not overhappy.
On Fortune's cap we are not the very button.

HAMLET

Nor the soles of her shoes?

ROSENCRANTZ
Neither, my lord.

HAMLET
Then you live about her waist, or in the middle of her favors?

GUILDENSTERN
Faith, her privates we.

HAMLET
In the secret parts of Fortune? Oh, most true. She is a strumpet. What news?

ROSENCRANTZ
None, my lord, but that the world's grown honest.

HAMLET
Then is doomsday near. But your news is not true. Let me question more in particular. What have you, my good friends, deserved at the hands of fortune that she sends you to prison hither?

GUILDENSTERN
Prison, my lord?

HAMLET
Denmark's a prison.

ROSENCRANTZ
Then is the world one.

HAMLET
A goodly one, in which there are many confines, wards, and dungeons, Denmark being one o' th' worst.

ROSENCRANTZ
We think not so, my lord.

HAMLET

Why, then, 'tis none to you, for there is nothing either good or bad, but thinking makes it so. To me it is a prison.

ROSENCRANTZ

Why then, your ambition makes it one. 'Tis too narrow for your mind.

HAMLET

O God, I could be bounded in a nutshell and count myself a king of infinite space, were it not that I have bad dreams.

GUILDENSTERN

Which dreams indeed are ambition, for the very substance of the ambitious is merely the shadow of a dream.

HAMLET

A dream itself is but a shadow.

ROSENCRANTZ

Truly, and I hold ambition of so airy and light a quality that it is but a shadow's shadow.

HAMLET

Then are our beggars bodies, and our monarchs and outstretched heroes the beggars' shadows. Shall we to th' court? For by my fay, I cannot reason.

ROSENCRANTZ, GUILDENSTERN

We'll wait upon you.

HAMLET

No such matter. I will not sort you with the rest of my servants, for, to speak to you like an honest man, I am most dreadfully attended. But in the beaten way of friendship, what make you at Elsinore?

ROSENCRANTZ

To visit you, my lord, no other occasion.

HAMLET

Beggar that I am, I am even poor in thanks; but I thank you, and sure, dear friends, my thanks are too dear a halfpenny. Were you not sent for? Is it your own inclining? Is it a free visitation? Come, come, deal justly with me. Come, come. Nay, speak.

GUILDENSTERN

What should we say, my lord?

HAMLET

Why, any thing, but to th' purpose. You were sent for, and there is a kind of confession in your looks which your modesties have not craft enough to color. I know the good king and queen have sent for you.

ROSENCRANTZ

To what end, my lord?

HAMLET

That you must teach me. But let me conjure you, by the rights of our fellowship, by the consonancy of our youth, by the obligation of our ever-preserved love, and by what more dear a better proposer could charge you withal: be even and direct with me whether you were sent for or no.

ROSENCRANTZ

(to GUILDENSTERN*)* What say you?

HAMLET

(aside) Nay, then, I have an eye of you—If you love me, hold not off.

GUILDENSTERN

My lord, we were sent for.

HAMLET

I will tell you why. So shall my anticipation prevent your discovery, and your secrecy to the king and queen moult no feather. I have of late—but wherefore I know not—lost all my mirth, forgone all custom of exercises, and indeed it goes so heavily with my disposition that this goodly frame, the earth, seems to me a sterile promontory; this most excellent canopy, the air—look you, this brave o'erhanging firmament, this majestical roof fretted with golden fire—why, it appears no other thing to me than a foul and pestilent congregation of vapors. What a piece of work is a man! How noble in reason, how infinite in faculty! In form and moving how express and admirable! In action how like an angel, in apprehension how like a god! The beauty of the world. The paragon of animals. And yet, to me, what is this quintessence of dust? Man delights not me. No, nor woman neither, though by your smiling you seem to say so.

ROSENCRANTZ

My lord, there was no such stuff in my thoughts.

HAMLET

Why did you laugh then, when I said "man delights not me"?

ROSENCRANTZ

To think, my lord, if you delight not in man, what Lenten entertainment the players shall receive from you. We coted them on the way, and hither are they coming to offer you service.

HAMLET

He that plays the king shall be welcome. His majesty shall have tribute of me. The adventurous knight shall use his foil and target, the lover shall not sigh gratis, the humorous man shall end

his part in peace, the clown shall make those laug
are tickle o' th' sear, and the lady shall say her min
blank verse shall halt for 't. What players are they?

ROSENCRANTZ

Even those you were wont to take delight in, the tragedians of
the city.

HAMLET

How chances it they travel? Their residence, both in reputation
and profit, was better both ways.

ROSENCRANTZ

I think their inhibition comes by the means of the late innovation.

HAMLET

Do they hold the same estimation they did when I was in the
city? Are they so followed?

ROSENCRANTZ

No, indeed are they not.

HAMLET

How comes it? Do they grow rusty?

ROSENCRANTZ

Nay, their endeavor keeps in the wonted pace. But there is,
sir, an eyrie of children, little eyases, that cry out on the top of
question and are most tyrannically clapped for 't. These are now
the fashion, and so berattle the common stages—so they call
them—that many wearing rapiers are afraid of goose quills and
dare scarce come thither.

HAMLET

What, are they children? Who maintains 'em? How are they
escoted? Will they pursue the quality no longer than they can

sing? Will they not say afterwards, if they should grow themselves to common players (as it is most like if their means are no better), their writers do them wrong to make them exclaim against their own succession?

ROSENCRANTZ
Faith, there has been much to do on both sides, and the nation holds it no sin to tar them to controversy. There was, for a while, no money bid for argument unless the poet and the player went to cuffs in the question.

HAMLET
Is 't possible?

GUILDENSTERN
Oh, there has been much throwing about of brains.

HAMLET
Do the boys carry it away?

ROSENCRANTZ
Ay, that they do, my lord. Hercules and his load too.

HAMLET
It is not very strange. For my uncle is King of Denmark, and those that would make mouths at him while my father lived give twenty, forty, fifty, a hundred ducats apiece for his picture in little. 'Sblood, there is something in this more than natural, if philosophy could find it out.

Flourish for the **PLAYERS** *within*

GUILDENSTERN
There are the players.

HAMLET

Gentlemen, you are welcome to Elsinore. Your har.
Th' appurtenance of welcome is fashion and cere
comply with you in this garb—lest my extent t
which, I tell you, must show fairly outwards, shoula more appear
like entertainment than yours. You are welcome. But my uncle-
father and aunt-mother are deceived.

GUILDENSTERN

In what, my dear lord?

HAMLET

I am but mad north-north-west. When the wind is southerly, I
know a hawk from a handsaw.

Enter POLONIUS

POLONIUS

Well be with you, gentlemen.

HAMLET

Hark you, Guildenstern, and you too—at each ear a hearer.
(indicates POLONIUS *)*That great baby you see there is not yet
out of his swaddling-clouts

ROSENCRANTZ

Happily he's the second time come to them, for they say an old
man is twice a child.

HAMLET

(aside to ROSENCRANTZ *and* GUILDENSTERN *)* I
will prophesy he comes to tell me of the players. Mark it. *(to*
POLONIUS*)*— You say right, sir. O' Monday morning, 'twas so
indeed.

POLONIUS
My lord, I have news to tell you.

HAMLET
My lord, I have news to tell you. When Roscius was an actor in Rome—

POLONIUS
The actors are come hither, my lord.

HAMLET
Buzz, buzz.

POLONIUS
Upon my honor—

HAMLET
Then came each actor on his ass—

POLONIUS
The best actors in the world, either for tragedy, comedy, history, pastoral, pastoral-comical, historical-pastoral, tragical-historical, tragical-comical-historical-pastoral, scene individable, or poem unlimited. Seneca cannot be too heavy, nor Plautus too light. For the law of writ and the liberty, these are the only men.

HAMLET
Jephthah, judge of Israel, what a treasure hadst thou!

POLONIUS
What a treasure had he, my lord?

HAMLET
Why,
One fair daughter and no more,
The which he lovèd passing well.

POLONIUS
(aside) Still on my daughter.

HAMLET
Am I not i' th' right, old Jephthah?

POLONIUS
If you call me Jephthah, my lord, I have a daughter that I love passing well.

HAMLET
Nay, that follows not.

POLONIUS
What follows, then, my lord?

HAMLET
Why,
As by lot, God wot, and then, you know,　*It came to pass, as most like it was*— The first row of the pious chanson will show you more, for look where my abridgement comes.

*Enter the **PLAYERS***

You are welcome, masters, welcome, all!—I am glad to see thee well.—Welcome, good friends.—O old friend? Why, thy face is valenced since I saw thee last. Comest thou to beard me in Denmark?—What, my young lady and mistress! By 'r Lady, your ladyship is nearer to heaven than when I saw you last, by the altitude of a chopine. Pray God, your voice, like a piece of uncurrent gold, be not cracked within the ring.—Masters, you are all welcome. We'll e'en to 't like French falconers, fly at any thing we see. We'll have a speech straight. Come, give us a taste of your quality. Come, a passionate speech.

FIRST PLAYER
What speech, my good lord?

HAMLET
I heard thee speak me a speech once, but it was never acted. Or, if it was, not above once, for the play, I remember, pleased not the million. 'Twas caviary to the general. But it was—as I received it, and others, whose judgments in such matters cried in the top of mine—an excellent play, well digested in the scenes, set down with as much modesty as cunning.

I remember, one said there were no sallets in the lines to make the matter savory, nor no matter in the phrase that might indict the author of affectation, but called it an honest method, as wholesome as sweet, and by very much more handsome than fine. One speech in it I chiefly loved. 'Twas Aeneas' tale to Dido and thereabout of it, especially where he speaks of Priam's slaughter. If it live in your >memory, begin at this line—Let me see, let me see—

The rugged Pyrrhus, like th' Hyrcanian beast—
It is not so. It begins with Pyrrhus—
The rugged Pyrrhus, he whose sable arms,
Black as his purpose, did the night resemble
When he lay couchèd in the ominous horse,
Hath now this dread and black complexion smeared
With heraldry more dismal. Head to foot
Now is he total gules, horridly tricked
With blood of fathers, mothers, daughters, sons,
Baked and impasted with the parching streets,
That lend a tyrannous and damnèd light
To their lord's murder. Roasted in wrath and fire,
And thus o'ersizèd with coagulate gore,
With eyes like carbuncles, the hellish Pyrrhus
Old grandsire Priam seeks.
So, proceed you.

POLONIUS

'Fore God, my lord, well spoken, with good accent and good discretion.

FIRST PLAYER

Anon he finds him
Striking too short at Greeks. His antique sword,
Rebellious to his arm, lies where it falls,
Repugnant to command. Unequal matched,
Pyrrhus at Priam drives, in rage strikes wide,
But with the whiff and wind of his fell sword
The unnerved father falls. Then senseless Ilium,
Seeming to feel this blow, with flaming top
Stoops to his base, and with a hideous crash
Takes prisoner Pyrrhus' ear. For, lo, his sword,
Which was declining on the milky head
Of reverend Priam, seemed i' th' air to stick.
So as a painted tyrant Pyrrhus stood,
And, like a neutral to his will and matter,
Did nothing.
But as we often see against some storm
A silence in the heavens, the rack stand still,
The bold winds speechless, and the orb below
As hush as death, anon the dreadful thunder
Doth rend the region. So, after Pyrrhus' pause,
Aroused vengeance sets him new a-work.
And never did the Cyclops' hammers fall
On Mars's armor forged for proof eterne
With less remorse than Pyrrhus' bleeding sword
Now falls on Priam.
Out, out, thou strumpet Fortune! All you gods
In general synod take away her power,
Break all the spokes and fellies from her wheel,
And bowl the round nave down the hill of heaven,
As low as to the fiends!

81

POLONIUS
This is too long.

HAMLET
It shall to the barber's, with your beard.—Prithee, say on. He's for a jig or a tale of bawdry, or he sleeps. Say on. Come to Hecuba.

FIRST PLAYER
But who, ah woe, who had seen the mobled queen—

HAMLET
"The mobled queen"?

POLONIUS
That's good. "Mobled queen" is good.

FIRST PLAYER
Run barefoot up and down, threatening the flames
With bisson rheum, a clout upon that head
Where late the diadem stood, and for a robe,
About her lank and all o'erteemèd loins,
A blanket, in the alarm of fear caught up—
Who this had seen, with tongue in venom steeped,
'Gainst fortune's state would treason have pronounced.
But if the gods themselves did see her then
When she saw Pyrrhus make malicious sport
In mincing with his sword her husband's limbs,
The instant burst of clamor that she made,
(Unless things mortal move them not at all)
Would have made milch the burning eyes of heaven,
And passion in the gods.

POLONIUS
Look whe'e he has not turned his color and has tears in 's eyes.—
Prithee, no more.

HAMLET

(to FIRST PLAYER*)* 'Tis well. I'll have thee speak out the rest soon. *(to* POLONIUS*)* Good my lord, will you see the players well bestowed? Do you hear, let them be well used, for they are the abstract and brief chronicles of the time. After your death you were better have a bad epitaph than their ill report while you live.

POLONIUS

My lord, I will use them according to their desert.

HAMLET

God's bodykins, man, much better. Use every man after his desert, and who should 'scape whipping? Use them after your own honor and dignity. The less they deserve, the more merit is in your bounty. Take them in.

POLONIUS

Come, sirs.

HAMLET

Follow him, friends. We'll hear a play tomorrow. *(to* FIRST PLAYER*)*— Dost thou hear me, old friend? Can you play *The Murder of Gonzago*?

FIRST PLAYER

Ay, my lord.

HAMLET

We'll ha 't tomorrow night. You could, for a need, study a speech of some dozen or sixteen lines which I would set down and insert in 't, could you not?

FIRST PLAYER

Ay, my lord.

HAMLET

Very well. Follow that lord, and look you mock him not.

*Exeunt **POLONIUS** and the **PLAYERS***

My good friends, I'll leave you till night. You are welcome to Elsinore.

ROSENCRANTZ

Good my lord.

HAMLET

Ay, so. Good-bye to you.

*Exeunt **ROSENCRANTZ** and **GUILDENSTERN***

Now I am alone.
Oh, what a rogue and peasant slave am I!
Is it not monstrous that this player here,
But in a fiction, in a dream of passion,
Could force his soul so to his own conceit
That from her working all his visage wanned,
Tears in his eyes, distraction in his aspect,
A broken voice, and his whole function suiting
With forms to his conceit? And all for nothing—
For Hecuba!
What's Hecuba to him or he to Hecuba
That he should weep for her? What would he do
Had he the motive and the cue for passion
That I have? He would drown the stage with tears
And cleave the general ear with horrid speech,
Make mad the guilty and appall the free,
Confound the ignorant, and amaze indeed

84

The very faculties of eyes and ears. Yet I,
A dull and muddy-mettled rascal, peak
Like John-a-dreams, unpregnant of my cau
And can say nothing—no, not for a king,
Upon whose property and most dear life
A damned defeat was made. Am I a coward?
Who calls me "villain"? Breaks my pate across?
Plucks off my beard and blows it in my face?
Tweaks me by the nose? Gives me the lie i' th' throat
As deep as to the lungs? Who does me this?
Ha!
'Swounds, I should take it, for it cannot be
But I am pigeon-livered and lack gall
To make oppression bitter, or ere this
I should have fatted all the region kites
With this slave's offal. Bloody, bawdy villain!
Remorseless, treacherous, lecherous, kindless villain!
O vengeance!
Why, what an ass am I! This is most brave,
That I, the son of a dear father murdered,
Prompted to my revenge by heaven and hell,
Must, like a whore, unpack my heart with words
And fall a-cursing like a very drab,
A scullion! Fie upon 't, foh!
About, my brain.—Hum, I have heard
That guilty creatures sitting at a play
Have, by the very cunning of the scene,
Been struck so to the soul that presently
They have proclaimed their malefactions.
For murder, though it have no tongue, will speak
With most miraculous organ. I'll have these players
Play something like the murder of my father
Before mine uncle. I'll observe his looks.
I'll tent him to the quick. If he do blench,

I know my course. The spirit that I have seen
May be the devil, and the devil hath power
T' assume a pleasing shape. Yea, and perhaps
Out of my weakness and my melancholy,
As he is very potent with such spirits,
Abuses me to damn me. I'll have grounds
More relative than this. The play's the thing
Wherein I'll catch the conscience of the king.

Exit

ACT 3

Scene 1

King. And can you, by no drift of circumstance,
Get from him why he puts on this confusion?
Act III. Scene I.

Claudius and Polonius hide and watch Hamlet as he debates suicide with himself. After Hamlet berates Ophelia, Claudius decides Hamlet may be dangerous and plans to send Hamlet off to England.

Enter *CLAUDIUS, GERTRUDE, POLONIUS, OPHELIA, ROSENCRANTZ, and GUILDENSTERN*

87

CLAUDIUS
And can you by no drift of circumstance
Get from him why he puts on this confusion,
Grating so harshly all his days of quiet
With turbulent and dangerous lunacy?

ROSENCRANTZ
He does confess he feels himself distracted.
But from what cause he will by no means speak.

GUILDENSTERN
Nor do we find him forward to be sounded.
But with a crafty madness keeps aloof
When we would bring him on to some confession
Of his true state.

GERTRUDE
Did he receive you well?

ROSENCRANTZ
Most like a gentleman.

GUILDENSTERN
But with much forcing of his disposition.

ROSENCRANTZ
Niggard of question, but of our demands
Most free in his reply.

GERTRUDE
Did you assay him?
To any pastime?

ROSENCRANTZ
Madam, it so fell out, that certain players
We o'erraught on the way. Of these we told him,

And there did seem in him a kind of joy
To hear of it. They are about the court,
And, as I think, they have already order
This night to play before him.

POLONIUS
'Tis most true,
And he beseeched me to entreat your Majesties
To hear and see the matter.

CLAUDIUS
With all my heart, and it doth much content me
To hear him so inclined.
Good gentlemen, give him a further edge,
And drive his purpose on to these delights.

ROSENCRANTZ
We shall, my lord.

*Exeunt **ROSENCRANTZ** and **GUILDENSTERN***

CLAUDIUS
Sweet Gertrude, leave us too,
For we have closely sent for Hamlet hither,
That he, as 'twere by accident, may here
Affront Ophelia.
Her father and myself (lawful espials)
Will so bestow ourselves that, seeing unseen,
We may of their encounter frankly judge,
And gather by him, as he is behaved,
If 't be the affliction of his love or no
That thus he suffers for.

GERTRUDE
I shall obey you.
And for your part, Ophelia, I do wish
That your good beauties be the happy cause
Of Hamlet's wildness. So shall I hope your virtues
Will bring him to his wonted way again,
To both your honors.

OPHELIA
Madam, I wish it may.

Exit **GERTRUDE**

POLONIUS
Ophelia, walk you here. *(to* CLAUDIUS*)* Gracious, so please you,
We will bestow ourselves. *(to* OPHELIA*)*Read on this book
That show of such an exercise may color
Your loneliness.—We are oft to blame in this,
'Tis too much proved, that with devotion's visage
And pious action we do sugar o'er
The devil himself.

CLAUDIUS
(aside)   Oh, 'tis too true!
How smart a lash that speech doth give my conscience!
The harlot's cheek, beautied with plastering art,
Is not more ugly to the thing that helps it
Than is my deed to my most painted word.
O heavy burden!

POLONIUS
I hear him coming. Let's withdraw, my lord.

CLAUDIUS and **POLONIUS** withdi

Enter **HAMLET**

HAMLET
To be, or not to be? That is the question—
Whether 'tis nobler in the mind to suffer
The slings and arrows of outrageous fortune,
Or to take arms against a sea of troubles,
And, by opposing, end them? To die, to sleep—
No more—and by a sleep to say we end
The heartache and the thousand natural shocks
That flesh is heir to—'tis a consummation
Devoutly to be wished! To die, to sleep.
To sleep, perchance to dream—ay, there's the rub,
For in that sleep of death what dreams may come
When we have shuffled off this mortal coil,
Must give us pause. There's the respect
That makes calamity of so long life.
For who would bear the whips and scorns of time,
Th' oppressor's wrong, the proud man's contumely,
The pangs of despised love, the law's delay,
The insolence of office, and the spurns
That patient merit of th' unworthy takes,
When he himself might his quietus make
With a bare bodkin? Who would fardels bear,
To grunt and sweat under a weary life,
But that the dread of something after death,
The undiscovered country from whose bourn
No traveler returns, puzzles the will
And makes us rather bear those ills we have
Than fly to others that we know not of?

91

Thus conscience does make cowards of us all,
And thus the native hue of resolution
Is sicklied o'er with the pale cast of thought,
And enterprises of great pith and moment
With this regard their currents turn awry,
And lose the name of action.—Soft you now,
The fair Ophelia!—Nymph, in thy orisons
Be all my sins remembered.

OPHELIA
Good my lord,
How does your honor for this many a day?

HAMLET
I humbly thank you. Well, well, well.

OPHELIA
My lord, I have remembrances of yours
That I have longèd long to redeliver.
I pray you now receive them.

HAMLET
No, not I. I never gave you aught.

OPHELIA
My honored lord, you know right well you did,
And with them, words of so sweet breath composed
As made the things more rich. Their perfume lost,
Take these again, for to the noble mind
Rich gifts wax poor when givers prove unkind.
There, my lord.

HAMLET
Ha, ha, are you honest?

OPHELIA
My lord?

HAMLET
Are you fair?

OPHELIA
What means your lordship?

HAMLET
That if you be honest and fair, your honesty should admit no discourse to your beauty.

OPHELIA
Could beauty, my lord, have better commerce than with honesty?

HAMLET
Ay, truly, for the power of beauty will sooner transform honesty from what it is to a bawd than the force of honesty can translate beauty into his likeness. This was sometime a paradox, but now the time gives it proof. I did love you once.

OPHELIA
Indeed, my lord, you made me believe so.

HAMLET

You should not have believed me, for virtue cannot so inoculate our old stock but we shall relish of it. I loved you not.

OPHELIA

I was the more deceived.

HAMLET

Get thee to a nunnery. Why wouldst thou be a breeder of sinners? I am myself indifferent honest, but yet I could accuse me of such things that it were better my mother had not borne me.

I am very proud, revengeful, ambitious, with more offences at my beck than I have thoughts to put them in, imagination to give them shape, or time to act them in. What should such fellows as I do crawling between earth and heaven? We are arrant knaves, all. Believe none of us. Go thy ways to a nunnery. Where's your father?

OPHELIA

At home, my lord.

HAMLET

Let the doors be shut upon him, that he may play the fool no where but in 's own house. Farewell.

OPHELIA

O, help him, you sweet heavens!

HAMLET

If thou dost marry, I'll give thee this plague for thy dowry. Be thou as chaste as ice, as pure as snow, thou shalt not escape calumny. Get thee to a nunnery, go. Farewell. Or, if thou wilt needs marry, marry a fool, for wise men know well enough what monsters you make of them. To a nunnery, go, and quickly too. Farewell.

OPHELIA

Heavenly powers, restore him!

HAMLET

I have heard of your paintings too, well enough. God has given you one face and you make yourselves another. You jig and amble, and you lisp, you nickname God's creatures and make your wantonness your ignorance. Go to, I'll no more on 't. It hath made me mad. I say, we will have no more marriages. Those that are married already, all but one, shall live. The rest shall keep as they are. To a nunnery, go.

Exit **HAMLET**

OPHELIA

Oh, what a noble mind is here o'erthrown!—
The courtier's, soldier's, scholar's, eye, tongue, sword,
Th' expectancy and rose of the fair state,
The glass of fashion and the mould of form,
Th' observed of all observers, quite, quite down!
And I, of ladies most deject and wretched,
That sucked the honey of his music vows,
Now see that noble and most sovereign reason
Like sweet bells jangled, out of tune and harsh;
That unmatched form and feature of blown youth
Blasted with ecstasy. Oh, woe is me,
T' have seen what I have seen, see what I see!

CLAUDIUS *and* **POLONIUS** *come forward*

CLAUDIUS

Love? His affections do not that way tend.
Nor what he spake, though it lacked form a little,

95

Was not like madness. There's something in his soul
O'er which his melancholy sits on brood,
And I do doubt the hatch and the disclose
Will be some danger—which for to prevent,
I have in quick determination
Thus set it down: he shall with speed to England
For the demand of our neglected tribute.
Haply the seas and countries different
With variable objects shall expel
This something-settled matter in his heart,
Whereon his brains still beating puts him thus
From fashion of himself. What think you on 't?

POLONIUS

It shall do well. But yet do I believe
The origin and commencement of his grief
Sprung from neglected love.—How now, Ophelia?
You need not tell us what Lord Hamlet said.
We heard it all.—My lord, do as you please.
But, if you hold it fit, after the play
Let his queen mother all alone entreat him
To show his grief. Let her be round with him,
And I'll be placed, so please you, in the ear
Of all their conference. If she find him not,
To England send him or confine him where
Your wisdom best shall think.

CLAUDIUS

It shall be so.
Madness in great ones must not unwatched go.

Exeunt

ACT 3

Scene 2

The actors perform a play that recreates Claudius's murder of his brother, causing Claudius to flee the room. Emboldened by this confirmation of Claudius's guilt, Hamlet goes to speak with Gertrude.

*Enter **HAMLET** and **PLAYERS***

HAMLET

Speak the speech, I pray you, as I pronounced it to you, trippingly on the tongue. But if you mouth it, as many of your players do, I had as lief the town crier spoke my lines. Nor do not saw the air too much with your hand thus, but use all gently, for in the very torrent, tempest, and (as I may say) whirlwind of passion, you must acquire and beget a temperance that may give it smoothness. Oh, it offends me to the soul to hear a robustious periwig-pated fellow tear a passion to tatters, to very rags, to split the ears of the groundlings, who for the most part are capable of nothing but inexplicable dumb-shows and noise. I would have such a fellow whipped for o'erdoing Termagant. It out-Herods Herod. Pray you, avoid it.

FIRST PLAYER

I warrant your honor.

HAMLET

Be not too tame neither, but let your own discretion be your tutor. Suit the action to the word, the word to the action, with this special observance that you o'erstep not the modesty of nature. For anything so overdone is from the purpose of playing, whose end, both at the first and now, was and is to hold, as 'twere, the mirror up to nature, to show virtue her own feature, scorn her own image, and the very age and body of the time his form and pressure. Now this overdone or come tardy off, though it make the unskillful laugh, cannot but make the judicious grieve, the censure of the which one must in your allowance o'erweigh a whole theatre of others.

Oh, there be players that I have seen play and heard others praise (and that highly), not to speak it profanely, that, neither having th' accent of Christians nor the gait of Christian, pagan, nor man, have so strutted and bellowed that I have thought some of nature's journeymen had made men and not made them well, they imitated humanity so abominably.

FIRST PLAYER
I hope we have reformed that indifferently with us, sir.

HAMLET
O, reform it altogether! And let those that play your clowns speak no more than is set down for them, for there be of them that will themselves laugh to set on some quantity of barren spectators to laugh too, though in the meantime some necessary question of the play be then to be considered. That's villainous, and shows a most pitiful ambition in the fool that uses it. Go, make you ready.

*Exeunt **PLAYERS***

*Enter **POLONIUS, ROSENCRANTZ,** and **GUILDENSTERN***

How now, my lord! Will the king hear this piece of work?

POLONIUS
And the queen too, and that presently.

HAMLET
Bid the players make haste.

*Exit **POLONIUS***

Will you two help to hasten them?

ROSENCRANTZ
Ay, my lord.

*Exeunt **ROSENCRANTZ** and **GUILDENSTERN***

HAMLET
What ho, Horatio!

*Enter **HORATIO***

HORATIO
Here, sweet lord, at your service.

HAMLET
Horatio, thou art e'en as just a man
As e'er my conversation coped withal.

HORATIO
O my dear lord—

HAMLET
Nay, do not think I flatter.
For what advancement may I hope from thee
That no revenue hast but thy good spirits,
To feed and clothe thee? Why should the poor be flattered?

No, let the candied tongue lick absurd pomp,
And crook the pregnant hinges of the knee
Where thrift may follow fawning. Dost thou hear?
Since my dear soul was mistress of her choice
And could of men distinguish, her election
Hath sealed thee for herself, for thou hast been—
As one in suffering all that suffers nothing—
A man that Fortune's buffets and rewards
Hast ta'en with equal thanks. And blessed are those
Whose blood and judgment are so well commingled,
That they are not a pipe for Fortune's finger
To sound what stop she please. Give me that man
That is not passion's slave, and I will wear him
In my heart's core, ay, in my heart of heart,
As I do thee.—Something too much of this.—
There is a play tonight before the king.
One scene of it comes near the circumstance
Which I have told thee of my father's death.
I prithee, when thou seest that act afoot,
Even with the very comment of thy soul
Observe mine uncle. If his occulted guilt
Do not itself unkennel in one speech,
It is a damnèd ghost that we have seen,
And my imaginations are as foul
As Vulcan's stithy. Give him heedful note.
For I mine eyes will rivet to his face,
And after we will both our judgments join
In censure of his seeming.

HORATIO
Well, my lord.
If he steal aught the whilst this play is playing,
And 'scape detecting, I will pay the theft.

100

*Danish march. Sound a flourish. Enter King **CLAUDIUS**, **Queen** **GERTRUDE**, **POLONIUS**, **OPHELIA**, **ROSENCRANTZ**, **GUILDENSTERN** and other lords attendant with **CLAUDIUS**'s; guard carrying torches*

HAMLET

They are coming to the play. I must be idle.
Get you a place.

CLAUDIUS

How fares our cousin Hamlet?

HAMLET

Excellent, i' faith, of the chameleon's dish. I eat the air, promise-crammed. You cannot feed capons so.

CLAUDIUS

I have nothing with this answer, Hamlet. These words are not mine.

HAMLET

No, nor mine now. *(to* POLONIUS*)* My lord, you played once i' th' university, you say?

POLONIUS

That did I, my lord, and was accounted a good actor.

HAMLET

What did you enact?

POLONIUS

I did enact Julius Caesar. I was killed i' th' Capitol. Brutus killed me.

HAMLET

It was a brute part of him to kill so capital a calf there.—Be the players ready?

ROSENCRANTZ

Ay, my lord. They stay upon your patience.

GERTRUDE

Come hither, my dear Hamlet, sit by me.

HAMLET

No, good mother. Here's metal more attractive. *(sits next to* OPHELIA*)*

POLONIUS

(to CLAUDIUS*)* Oh, ho, do you mark that?

HAMLET

Lady, shall I lie in your lap?

OPHELIA

No, my lord.

HAMLET

I mean, my head upon your lap?

OPHELIA

Ay, my lord.

HAMLET

Do you think I meant country matters?

OPHELIA

I think nothing, my lord.

HAMLET

That's a fair thought to lie between maids' legs.

OPHELIA
What is, my lord?

HAMLET
Nothing.

OPHELIA
You are merry, my lord.

HAMLET
Who, I?

OPHELIA
Ay, my lord.

HAMLET
O God, your only jig-maker. What should a man do but be merry? For, look you, how cheerfully my mother looks, and my father died within these two hours.

OPHELIA
Nay, 'tis twice two months, my lord.

HAMLET
So long? Nay then, let the devil wear black, for I'll have a suit of sables. O heavens! Die two months ago and not forgotten yet? Then there's hope a great man's memory may outlive his life half a year. But, by 'r Lady, he must build churches then, or else shall he suffer not thinking on, with the hobby-horse, whose epitaph is "For, oh, for, oh, the hobby-horse is forgot."
Trumpets sound. The dumb show begins
Enter a King and a Queen very lovingly, the Queen embracing him and he her. She kneels and makes show of protestation unto him. He takes her up and declines his head upon her neck, lays him down upon a bank of flowers. She, seeing him asleep, leaves him. Anon

comes in a fellow, takes off his crown, kisses it, pours poison in the King's ears, and exits. The Queen returns, finds the King dead, and makes passionate action. The Poisoner, with some two or three Mutes, comes in again, seeming to lament with her. The dead body is carried away. The Poisoner woos the Queen with gifts. She seems loath and unwilling awhile, but in the end accepts his love

Exeunt **PLAYERS**

OPHELIA
What means this, my lord?

HAMLET
Marry, this is miching *malhecho*. It means mischief.

OPHELIA
Belike this show imports the argument of the play.

Enter **PROLOGUE**

HAMLET
We shall know by this fellow. The players cannot keep counsel. They'll tell all.

OPHELIA
Will he tell us what this show meant?

HAMLET
Ay, or any show that you will show him. Be not you ashamed to show, he'll not shame to tell you what it means.

OPHELIA
You are naught, you are naught. I'll mark the play.

PROLOGUE
For us and for our tragedy,
Here stooping to your clemency,
We beg your hearing patiently.

*Exit **PROLOGUE***

HAMLET
Is this a prologue or the posy of a ring?

OPHELIA
'Tis brief, my lord.

HAMLET
As woman's love.

*Enter **PLAYER KING** and **PLAYER QUEEN***

PLAYER KING

Full thirty times hath Phoebus' cart gone round
Neptune's salt wash and Tellus' orbèd ground,
And thirty dozen moons with borrowed sheen
About the world have times twelve thirties been,
Since love our hearts and Hymen did our hands
Unite commutual in most sacred bands.

PLAYER QUEEN
So many journeys may the sun and moon
Make us again count o'er ere love be done.
But woe is me! You are so sick of late,
So far from cheer and from your former state,

105

That I distrust you. Yet though I distrust,
Discomfort you, my lord, it nothing must.
For women fear too much, even as they love,
And women's fear and love hold quantity,
In neither aught, or in extremity.
Now what my love is, proof hath made you know,
And as my love is sized, my fear is so:
Where love is great, the littlest doubts are fear.
Where little fears grow great, great love grows there.

PLAYER KING

Faith, I must leave thee, love, and shortly too.
My operant powers their functions leave to do.
And thou shalt live in this fair world behind,
Honored, beloved, and haply one as kind
For husband shalt thou—

PLAYER QUEEN

Oh, confound the rest!
Such love must needs be treason in my breast.
In second husband let me be accursed!
None wed the second but who killed the first.

HAMLET

(aside)Wormwood, wormwood.

PLAYER QUEEN

The instances that second marriage move
Are base respects of thrift, but none of love.
A second time I kill my husband dead
When second husband kisses me in bed.

PLAYER KING

I do believe you think what now you speak,
But what we do determine oft we break.

106

Purpose is but the slave to memory,
Of violent birth, but poor validity,
Which now, like fruit unripe, sticks on the tree,
But fall, unshaken, when they mellow be.
Most necessary 'tis that we forget
To pay ourselves what to ourselves is debt.
What to ourselves in passion we propose,
The passion ending, doth the purpose lose.
The violence of either grief or joy
Their own enactures with themselves destroy.
Where joy most revels, grief doth most lament.
Grief joys, joy grieves on slender accident.
This world is not for aye, nor 'tis not strange
That even our loves should with our fortunes change.
For 'tis a question left us yet to prove,
Whether love lead fortune, or else fortune love.
The great man down, you mark his favorite flies.
The poor advanced makes friends of enemies.
And hitherto doth love on fortune tend,
For who not needs shall never lack a friend,
And who in want a hollow friend doth try,
Directly seasons him his enemy.
But, orderly to end where I begun,
Our wills and fates do so contrary run
That our devices still are overthrown.
Our thoughts are ours, their ends none of our own.
So think thou wilt no second husband wed,
But die thy thoughts when thy first lord is dead.

PLAYER QUEEN

Nor earth to me give food, nor heaven light.
Sport and repose lock from me day and night.
To desperation turn my trust and hope.
An anchor's cheer in prison be my scope.

107

Each opposite that blanks the face of joy
Meet what I would have well and it destroy.
Both here and hence pursue me lasting strife
If, once a widow, ever I be wife!

HAMLET
If she should break it now!

PLAYER KING
'Tis deeply sworn. Sweet, leave me here awhile.
My spirits grow dull, and fain I would beguile
The tedious day with sleep.

*The **PLAYER KING** sleeps*

PLAYER QUEEN
Sleep rock thy brain,
And never come mischance between us twain.

*Exit **PLAYER QUEEN***

HAMLET
Madam, how like you this play?

GERTRUDE
The lady protests too much, methinks.

HAMLET
Oh, but she'll keep her word.

CLAUDIUS
Have you heard the argument? Is there no offense in 't?

HAMLET
No, no, they do but jest. Poison in jest. No offense i' th' world.

CLAUDIUS

What do you call the play?

HAMLET

The Mousetrap. Marry, how? Tropically. This play is the image of a murder done in Vienna. Gonzago is the duke's name, his wife Baptista. You shall see anon. 'Tis a knavish piece of work, but what o' that? Your majesty and we that have free souls, it touches us not. Let the galled jade wince, our withers are unwrung.

*Enter **LUCIANUS***

This is one Lucianus, nephew to the king.

OPHELIA

You are as good as a chorus, my lord.

HAMLET

I could interpret between you and your love, if I could see the puppets dallying.

OPHELIA

You are keen, my lord, you are keen.

HAMLET

It would cost you a groaning to take off mine edge.

OPHELIA

Still better and worse.

HAMLET

So you must take your husbands.—Begin, murderer. Pox, leave thy damnable faces, and begin. Come, "The croaking raven doth bellow for revenge—"

LUCIANUS

Thoughts black, hands apt, drugs fit, and time agreeing,
Confederate season, else no creature seeing,
Thou mixture rank, of midnight weeds collected,
With Hecate's ban thrice blasted, thrice infected,
Thy natural magic and dire property
On wholesome life usurp immediately.
(pours poison into PLAYER KING *'s ears)*

HAMLET

He poisons him i' th' garden for 's estate. His name's Gonzago. The story is extant, and writ in choice Italian. You shall see anon how the murderer gets the love of Gonzago's wife.

CLAUDIUS *stands up*

OPHELIA
The king rises.

HAMLET
What, frighted with false fire?

GERTRUDE
How fares my lord?

POLONIUS
Give o'er the play.

CLAUDIUS
Give me some light, away!

POLONIUS
Lights, lights, lights!

*Commotion. Exeunt all but **HAMLET** and **HORATIO***

HAMLET
Why, let the stricken deer go weep,
The hart ungallèd play.
For some must watch while some must sleep.
So runs the world away.
Would not this, sir, and a forest of feathers—if the rest of my fortunes turn Turk with me—with two Provincial roses on my razed shoes, get me a fellowship in a cry of players?

HORATIO
Half a share.

HAMLET
A whole one, I.
For thou dost know, O Damon dear,
This realm dismantled was

111

Of Jove himself. And now reigns here
A very, very—pajock.

HORATIO
You might have rhymed.

HAMLET
O good Horatio, I'll take the ghost's word for a thousand pound.
Didst perceive?

HORATIO
Very well, my lord.

HAMLET
Upon the talk of the poisoning?

HORATIO
I did very well note him.

HAMLET
Ah ha! Come, some music! Come, the recorders!
For if the king like not the comedy,
Why then, belike, he likes it not, perdy.
Come, some music!

Enter **ROSENCRANTZ** *and* **GUILDENSTERN**

GUILDENSTERN
Good my lord, vouchsafe me a word with you.

HAMLET
Sir, a whole history.

GUILDENSTERN
The king, sir—

HAMLET

Ay, sir, what of him?

GUILDENSTERN

Is in his retirement marvelous distempered.

HAMLET

With drink, sir?

GUILDENSTERN

No, my lord, with choler.

HAMLET

Your wisdom should show itself more richer to signify this to the doctor. For, for me to put him to his purgation would perhaps plunge him into far more choler.

GUILDENSTERN

Good my lord, put your discourse into some frame and start not so wildly from my affair.

HAMLET

I am tame, sir. Pronounce.

GUILDENSTERN

The queen your mother, in most great affliction of spirit, hath sent me to you.

HAMLET

You are welcome.

GUILDENSTERN

Nay, good my lord, this courtesy is not of the right breed. If it shall please you to make me a wholesome answer, I will do your mother's commandment. If not, your pardon and my return shall be the end of my business.

HAMLET
Sir, I cannot.

GUILDENSTERN
What, my lord?

HAMLET
Make you a wholesome answer. My wit's diseased. But, sir, such answer as I can make, you shall command. Or, rather, as you say, my mother. Therefore no more but to the matter. My mother, you say—

ROSENCRANTZ
Then thus she says: your behavior hath struck her into amazement and admiration.

HAMLET
O wonderful son that can so 'stonish a mother! But is there no sequel at the heels of this mother's admiration? Impart.

ROSENCRANTZ
She desires to speak with you in her closet ere you go to bed.

HAMLET
We shall obey, were she ten times our mother. Have you any further trade with us?

ROSENCRANTZ
My lord, you once did love me.

HAMLET
And do still, by these pickers and stealers.

ROSENCRANTZ
Good my lord, what is your cause of distemper? You do surely bar the door upon your own liberty if you deny your griefs to your friend.

HAMLET

Sir, I lack advancement.

ROSENCRANTZ

How can that be, when you have the voice of the king himself for your succession in Denmark?

*Reenter the **PLAYERS** with recorders*

HAMLET

Ay, sir, but "While the grass grows—" The proverb is something musty—Oh, the recorders! Let me see one. *(takes a recorder) (aside to* ROSENCRANTZ *and* GUILDENSTERN *)* To withdraw with you, why do you go about to recover the wind of me as if you would drive me into a toil?

GUILDENSTERN

O my lord, if my duty be too bold, my love is too unmannerly.

HAMLET

I do not well understand that. Will you play upon this pipe?

GUILDENSTERN

My lord, I cannot.

HAMLET

I pray you.

GUILDENSTERN

Believe me, I cannot.

HAMLET

I do beseech you.

GUILDENSTERN

I know no touch of it, my lord.

HAMLET

It is as easy as lying. Govern these ventages with your fingers and thumb, give it breath with your mouth, and it will discourse most eloquent music. Look you, these are the stops.

GUILDENSTERN

But these cannot I command to any utterance of harmony. I have not the skill.

HAMLET

Why, look you now, how unworthy a thing you make of me! You would play upon me. You would seem to know my stops. You would pluck out the heart of my mystery. You would sound me from my lowest note to the top of my compass. And there is much music, excellent voice, in this little organ, yet cannot you make it speak? 'Sblood, do you think I am easier to be played on than a pipe? Call me what instrument you will, though you can fret me, yet you cannot play upon me.

Enter POLONIUS

God bless you, sir.

POLONIUS

My lord, the queen would speak with you, and presently.

HAMLET

Do you see yonder cloud that's almost in shape of a camel?

POLONIUS

By th' mass, and 'tis like a camel indeed.

HAMLET

Methinks it is like a weasel.

POLONIUS

It is backed like a weasel.

HAMLET

Or like a whale.

POLONIUS

Very like a whale.

HAMLET

Then I will come to my mother by and by. *(aside)* They fool me to the top of my bent.—I will come by and by.

POLONIUS

I will say so.

HAMLET

"By and by" is easily said.

*Exit **POLONIUS***

Leave me, friends.

*Exeunt all but **HAMLET***

'Tis now the very witching time of night,
When churchyards yawn and hell itself breathes out
Contagion to this world. Now could I drink hot blood
And do such bitter business as the bitter day
Would quake to look on. Soft, now to my mother.—
O heart, lose not thy nature, let not ever

The soul of Nero enter this firm bosom.
Let me be cruel, not unnatural.
will speak daggers to her but use none.
My tongue and soul in this be hypocrites.
How in my words somever she be shent,
To give them seals never, my soul, consent!

Exit

ACT 3

Scene 3

Polonius plans to eavesdrop on Hamlet and Gertrude. Hamlet sees Claudius praying and considers killing him, but worries that if he kills Claudius while he seeks forgiveness, Claudius might go to heaven.

*Enter **CLAUDIUS, ROSENCRANTZ,** and **GUILDENSTERN***

CLAUDIUS
I like him not, nor stands it safe with us
To let his madness range. Therefore prepare you.
I your commission will forthwith dispatch,
And he to England shall along with you.
The terms of our estate may not endure
Hazard so dangerous as doth hourly grow
Out of his lunacies.

GUILDENSTERN
We will ourselves provide.
Most holy and religious fear it is
To keep those many, many bodies safe
That live and feed upon your majesty.

ROSENCRANTZ
The single and peculiar life is bound
With all the strength and armor of the mind
To keep itself from noyance, but much more

119

That spirit upon whose weal depend and rest
15 The lives of many. The cease of majesty
Dies not alone, but, like a gulf, doth draw
What's near it with it. It is a massy wheel
Fixed on the summit of the highest mount,
To whose huge spokes ten thousand lesser things
Are mortised and adjoined, which, when it falls,
Each small annexment, petty consequence,
Attends the boisterous ruin. Never alone
Did the king sigh, but with a general groan.

CLAUDIUS
Arm you, I pray you, to this speedy voyage.
For we will fetters put upon this fear,
Which now goes too free-footed.

ROSENCRANTZ, GUILDENSTERN
We will haste us.

Exeunt ROSENCRANTZ and GUILDENSTERN

Enter POLONIUS

POLONIUS
My lord, he's going to his mother's closet.
Behind the arras I'll convey myself
To hear the process. I'll warrant she'll tax him home.
And, as you said (and wisely was it said)
'Tis meet that some more audience than a mother—
Since nature makes them partial—should o'erhear
The speech, of vantage. Fare you well, my liege.
I'll call upon you ere you go to bed
And tell you what I know.

CLAUDIUS
Thanks, dear my lord.

*Exit **POLONIUS***

Oh, my offence is rank. It smells to heaven.
It hath the primal eldest curse upon 't,
A brother's murder. Pray can I not.
Though inclination be as sharp as will,
My stronger guilt defeats my strong intent,
And, like a man to double business bound,
I stand in pause where I shall first begin,
And both neglect. What if this cursèd hand
Were thicker than itself with brother's blood?
Is there not rain enough in the sweet heavens
To wash it white as snow? Whereto serves mercy
But to confront the visage of offence?
And what's in prayer but this twofold force,
To be forestallèd ere we come to fall
Or pardoned being down? Then I'll look up.
My fault is past. But oh, what form of prayer
Can serve my turn, "Forgive me my foul murder"?
That cannot be, since I am still possessed
Of those effects for which I did the murder:
My crown, mine own ambition, and my queen.
May one be pardoned and retain th' offense?
In the corrupted currents of this world
Offense's gilded hand may shove by justice,
And oft 'tis seen the wicked prize itself
Buys out the law. But 'tis not so above.
There is no shuffling. There the action lies
In his true nature, and we ourselves compelled,
Even to the teeth and forehead of our faults,

To give in evidence. What then? What rests?
Try what repentance can. What can it not?
Yet what can it when one can not repent?
O wretched state! O bosom black as death!
O limèd soul that, struggling to be free,
Art more engaged! Help, angels. Make assay.
Bow, stubborn knees, and, heart with strings of steel,
Be soft as sinews of the newborn babe.
All may be well. *(kneels)*

Enter **HAMLET**

HAMLET
Now might I do it pat. Now he is a-praying.
And now I'll do 't. And so he goes to heaven.
And so am I revenged.—That would be scanned.
A villain kills my father, and, for that,
I, his sole son, do this same villain send
To heaven.
Oh, this is hire and salary, not revenge.
He took my father grossly, full of bread,
With all his crimes broad blown, as flush as May.
And how his audit stands who knows save heaven?
But in our circumstance and course of thought
'Tis heavy with him. And am I then revenged
To take him in the purging of his soul
When he is fit and seasoned for his passage?
No.
Up, sword, and know thou a more horrid hent.
When he is drunk asleep, or in his rage,
Or in th' incestuous pleasure of his bed,
At game a-swearing, or about some act
That has no relish of salvation in 't—

Then trip him, that his heels may kick at heaven,
And that his soul may be as damned and black
As hell, whereto it goes. My mother stays
This physic but prolongs thy sickly days.

Exit **HAMLET**

CLAUDIUS
(rises) My words fly up, my thoughts remain below.
Words without thoughts never to heaven go.

Exit

ACT 3

Scene 4

Hamlet confronts Gertrude, and when he sees someone hiding behind the curtains, Hamlet stabs and kills Polonius, thinking he is Claudius. The ghost reminds Hamlet that he still hasn't killed Claudius.

*Enter **GERTRUDE** and **POLONIUS***

POLONIUS
He will come straight. Look you lay home to him.
Tell him his pranks have been too broad to bear with,
And that your grace hath screened and stood between
Much heat and him. I'll silence me even here.
Pray you, be round with him.

HAMLET
(within) Mother, mother, mother!

GERTRUDE
I'll warrant you. Fear me not. Withdraw, I hear him coming.

***POLONIUS** hides behind the arras*

*Enter **HAMLET***

HAMLET
Now mother, what's the matter?

GERTRUDE
Hamlet, thou hast thy father much offended.

HAMLET
Mother, you have my father much offended.

GERTRUDE
Come, come, you answer with an idle tongue.

HAMLET
Go, go, you question with a wicked tongue.

GERTRUDE
Why, how now, Hamlet?

HAMLET
What's the matter now?

GERTRUDE
Have you forgot me?

HAMLET
No, by the rood, not so.
You are the queen, your husband's brother's wife,
And—would it were not so!—you are my mother.

GERTRUDE
Nay, then I'll set those to you that can speak.

HAMLET
Come, come, and sit you down. You shall not budge.
You go not till I set you up a glass
Where you may see the inmost part of you.

GERTRUDE
What wilt thou do? Thou wilt not murder me?
Help, help, ho!

POLONIUS

(from behind the arras) What, ho? Help, help, help!

HAMLET

How now, a rat? Dead for a ducat, dead!
*(stabs his sword through the arras and kills **POLONIUS**)*

POLONIUS

(from behind the arras) Oh, I am slain.

GERTRUDE

O me, what hast thou done?

HAMLET

Nay, I know not. Is it the king?

GERTRUDE

Oh, what a rash and bloody deed is this!

HAMLET

A bloody deed? Almost as bad, good mother,
As kill a king and marry with his brother.

GERTRUDE

As kill a king?

HAMLET

Ay, lady, 'twas my word.
*(draws back the arras and discovers **POLONIUS**)*
Thou wretched, rash, intruding fool, farewell.
I took thee for thy better. Take thy fortune.
Thou find'st to be too busy is some danger.
(to GERTRUDE*)* Leave wringing of your hands. Peace. Sit you down
And let me wring your heart. For so I shall
If it be made of penetrable stuff,

127

If damnèd custom have not brassed it so
That it is proof and bulwark against sense.

GERTRUDE
What have I done, that thou darest wag thy tongue
In noise so rude against me?

HAMLET
Such an act
That blurs the grace and blush of modesty,
Calls virtue hypocrite, takes off the rose
From the fair forehead of an innocent love
And sets a blister there, makes marriage vows
As false as dicers' oaths—oh, such a deed
As from the body of contraction plucks
The very soul, and sweet religion makes
A rhapsody of words. Heaven's face doth glow
O'er this solidity and compound mass
With tristful visage, as against the doom,
Is thought-sick at the act.

GERTRUDE
Ay me, what act
That roars so loud and thunders in the index?

HAMLET
Look here upon this picture and on this,
The counterfeit presentment of two brothers.
See, what a grace was seated on this brow?
Hyperion's curls, the front of Jove himself,
An eye like Mars to threaten and command,
A station like the herald Mercury
New-lighted on a heaven-kissing hill—
A combination and a form indeed
Where every god did seem to set his seal

To give the world assurance of a man.
This was your husband. Look you now, what follows.
Here is your husband, like a mildewed ear
Blasting his wholesome brother. Have you eyes?
Could you on this fair mountain leave to feed
And batten on this moor? Ha, have you eyes?
You cannot call it love, for at your age
The heyday in the blood is tame, it's humble,
And waits upon the judgment. And what judgment
Would step from this to this? Sense sure you have,
Else could you not have motion. But sure that sense
Is apoplexed, for madness would not err,
Nor sense to ecstasy was ne'er so thralled,
But it reserved some quantity of choice
To serve in such a difference. What devil was 't
That thus hath cozened you at hoodman-blind?
Eyes without feeling, feeling without sight,
Ears without hands or eyes, smelling sans all,
Or but a sickly part of one true sense
Could not so mope. O shame, where is thy blush?
Rebellious hell,
If thou canst mutine in a matron's bones,
To flaming youth let virtue be as wax
And melt in her own fire. Proclaim no shame
When the compulsive ardor gives the charge,
Since frost itself as actively doth burn,
And reason panders will.

GERTRUDE
O Hamlet, speak no more!
Thou turn'st mine eyes into my very soul,
And there I see such black and grainèd spots
As will not leave their tinct.

HAMLET
Nay, but to live
In the rank sweat of an enseamèd bed,
Stewed in corruption, honeying and making love
Over the nasty sty—

GERTRUDE
O, speak to me no more!
These words like daggers enter in my ears.
No more, sweet Hamlet.

HAMLET
A murderer and a villain,
A slave that is not twentieth part the tithe
Of your precedent lord, a vice of kings,
A cutpurse of the empire and the rule,
That from a shelf the precious diadem stole,
And put it in his pocket—

GERTRUDE
No more!

HAMLET
A king of shreds and patches—

Enter **GHOST**

Save me and hover o'er me with your wings,
You heavenly guards!—What would your gracious figure?

GERTRUDE
Alas, he's mad!

HAMLET
Do you not come your tardy son to chide,

That, lapsed in time and passion, lets go by
The important acting of your dread command?
O, say!

GHOST

Do not forget. This visitation
Is but to whet thy almost blunted purpose.
But look, amazement on thy mother sits.
O, step between her and her fighting soul.
Conceit in weakest bodies strongest works.
Speak to her, Hamlet.

HAMLET

How is it with you, lady?

GERTRUDE

Alas, how is 't with you,
That you do bend your eye on vacancy
And with th' incorporal air do hold discourse?
Forth at your eyes your spirits wildly peep,
And, as the sleeping soldiers in th' alarm,
Your bedded hair, like life in excrements,
Starts up and stands on end. O gentle son,
Upon the heat and flame of thy distemper
Sprinkle cool patience. Whereon do you look?

HAMLET

On him, on him! Look you, how pale he glares!
His form and cause conjoined, preaching to stones,
Would make them capable.
(to GHOST*)* Do not look upon me,
Lest with this piteous action you convert
My stern effects. Then what I have to do
Will want true color—tears perchance for blood.

GERTRUDE
To whom do you speak this?

HAMLET
Do you see nothing there?

GERTRUDE
Nothing at all, yet all that is I see.

HAMLET
Nor did you nothing hear?

GERTRUDE
No, nothing but ourselves.

HAMLET
Why, look you there! Look how it steals away—
My father, in his habit as he lived—
Look where he goes, even now, out at the portal!

Exit **GHOST**

GERTRUDE
This the very coinage of your brain.
This bodiless creation ecstasy
Is very cunning in.

HAMLET
Ecstasy?
My pulse as yours doth temperately keep time
And makes as healthful music. It is not madness
That I have uttered. Bring me to the test,
And I the matter will reword, which madness
Would gambol from. Mother, for love of grace,

Lay not that flattering unction to your soul
That not your trespass but my madness speaks.
It will but skin and film the ulcerous place
Whilst rank corruption, mining all within,
Infects unseen. Confess yourself to heaven.
Repent what's past. Avoid what is to come.
And do not spread the compost on the weeds
To make them ranker. Forgive me this my virtue,
For in the fatness of these pursy times
Virtue itself of vice must pardon beg,
Yea, curb and woo for leave to do him good.

GERTRUDE
O Hamlet, thou hast cleft my heart in twain.

HAMLET
Oh, throw away the worser part of it,
And live the purer with the other half.
Good night—but go not to mine uncle's bed.
Assume a virtue if you have it not.
That monster, custom, who all sense doth eat,
Of habits devil, is angel yet in this:
That to the use of actions fair and good
He likewise gives a frock or livery
That aptly is put on. Refrain tonight,
And that shall lend a kind of easiness
To the next abstinence, the next more easy.
For use almost can change the stamp of nature,
And either rein the devil or throw him out
With wondrous potency. Once more, good night,
And when you are desirous to be blessed,
I'll blessing beg of you. *(points to* POLONIUS*)*
For this same lord,
I do repent. But heaven hath pleased it so,

To punish me with this and this with me,
That I must be their scourge and minister.
I will bestow him and will answer well
The death I gave him. So, again, good night.
I must be cruel only to be kind.
Thus bad begins and worse remains behind.
One word more, good lady—

GERTRUDE
What shall I do?

HAMLET
Not this, by no means, that I bid you do—
Let the bloat king tempt you again to bed,
Pinch wanton on your cheek, call you his mouse,
And let him, for a pair of reechy kisses
Or paddling in your neck with his damned fingers,
Make you to ravel all this matter out:
That I essentially am not in madness
But mad in craft. 'Twere good you let him know,
For who that's but a queen, fair, sober, wise,
Would from a paddock, from a bat, a gib,
Such dear concernings hide? Who would do so?
No, in despite of sense and secrecy,
Unpeg the basket on the house's top.
Let the birds fly, and like the famous ape,
To try conclusions, in the basket creep
And break your own neck down.

GERTRUDE
Be thou assured, if words be made of breath
And breath of life, I have no life to breathe
What thou hast said to me.

HAMLET
I must to England, you know that?

GERTRUDE
Alack,
I had forgot. 'Tis so concluded on.

HAMLET
There's letters sealed, and my two schoolfellows,
Whom I will trust as I will adders fanged,
They bear the mandate. They must sweep my way
And marshal me to knavery. Let it work,
For 'tis the sport to have the engineer
Hoist with his own petard. And 't shall go hard,
But I will delve one yard below their mines,
And blow them at the moon. Oh, 'tis most sweet
When in one line two crafts directly meet.
(indicates POLONIUS *)*
This man shall set me packing.
I'll lug the guts into the neighbor room.
Mother, good night. Indeed this counselor
Is now most still, most secret, and most grave
Who was in life a foolish prating knave.—
Come, sir, to draw toward an end with you.—
Good night, mother.

Exeunt, **HAMLET** *tugging in* **POLONIUS**

ACT 4

Scene 1

Gertrude tells Claudius about the murder of Polonius, and Claudius determines that they must ship Hamlet off to England immediately. Rosencrantz and Guildenstern are sent to find Hamlet.

*Enter King **CLAUDIUS** and Queen **GERTRUDE**, with **ROSENCRANTZ** and **GUILDENSTERN***

CLAUDIUS
(to GERTRUDE*)* There's matter in these sighs, these profound heaves.
You must translate. 'Tis fit we understand them.
Where is your son?

GERTRUDE
(to ROSENCRANTZ *and* GUILDENSTERN*)*
Bestow this place on us a little while.

*Exeunt **ROSENCRANTZ** and **GUILDENSTERN***

Ah, my good lord, what have I seen tonight!

CLAUDIUS
What, Gertrude? How does Hamlet?

GERTRUDE

Mad as the sea and wind when both contend
Which is the mightier. In his lawless fit,
Behind the arras hearing something stir,
Whips out his rapier, cries, "A rat, a rat!"
And in this brainish apprehension kills
The unseen good old man.

CLAUDIUS

O heavy deed!
It had been so with us, had we been there.
His liberty is full of threats to all—
To you yourself, to us, to everyone.
Alas, how shall this bloody deed be answered?
It will be laid to us, whose providence
Should have kept short, restrained and out of haunt,
This mad young man. But so much was our love,
We would not understand what was most fit,
But, like the owner of a foul disease,
To keep it from divulging, let it feed
Even on the pith of life. Where is he gone?

GERTRUDE

To draw apart the body he hath killed,
O'er whom his very madness, like some ore
Among a mineral of metals base,
Shows itself pure. He weeps for what is done.

CLAUDIUS

O Gertrude, come away!
The sun no sooner shall the mountains touch
But we will ship him hence, and this vile deed
We must, with all our majesty and skill,
Both countenance and excuse.—Ho, Guildenstern!

*Enter **ROSENCRANTZ** and **GUILDENSTERN***

Friends both, go join you with some further aid.
Hamlet in madness hath Polonius slain,
And from his mother's closet hath he dragged him.
Go seek him out, speak fair, and bring the body
Into the chapel. I pray you, haste in this.

*Exeunt **ROSENCRANTZ** and **GUILDENSTERN***

Come, Gertrude, we'll call up our wisest friends,
And let them know both what we mean to do
And what's untimely done. So dreaded slander—
Whose whisper o'er the world's diameter,
As level as the cannon to his blank,
Transports the poisoned shot—may miss our name
And hit the woundless air. Oh, come away!
My soul is full of discord and dismay.

Exeunt

ACT 4

Scene 2

Rosencrantz and Guildenstern find Hamlet, but he refuses to tell them where he has hidden Polonius's body, accusing them of being spies for Claudius.

Enter **HAMLET**

HAMLET
Safely stowed.

GENTLEMEN
(from within) Hamlet! Lord Hamlet!

HAMLET
But soft, what noise? Who calls on Hamlet?
Oh, here they come.

Enter **ROSENCRANTZ, GUILDENSTERN**, *and others*

ROSENCRANTZ
What have you done, my lord, with the dead body?

HAMLET
Compounded it with dust, whereto 'tis kin.

ROSENCRANTZ

Tell us where 'tis, that we may take it thence
And bear it to the chapel.

HAMLET

Do not believe it.

ROSENCRANTZ

Believe what?

HAMLET

That I can keep your counsel and not mine own. Besides, to be demanded of a sponge! What replication should be made by the son of a king?

ROSENCRANTZ

Take you me for a sponge, my lord?

HAMLET

Ay, sir, that soaks up the king's countenance, his rewards, his authorities. But such officers do the king best service in the end. He keeps them, like an ape, in the corner of his jaw, first mouthed to be last swallowed. When he needs what you have gleaned, it is but squeezing you and, sponge, you shall be dry again.

ROSENCRANTZ

I understand you not, my lord.

HAMLET

I am glad of it. A knavish speech sleeps in a foolish ear.

ROSENCRANTZ

My lord, you must tell us where the body is and go with us to the king.

HAMLET

The body is with the king, but the king is not with the body.
The king is a thing—

GUILDENSTERN

A thing, my lord?

HAMLET

Of nothing. Bring me to him. Hide, fox, and all after.

Exeunt

ACT 4

Scene 3

Claudius questions Hamlet until Hamlet reveals the location of Polonius's body. Claudius sends Hamlet away to England, accompanied by Rosencrantz and Guildenstern, and with secret orders for Hamlet to be put to death when he arrives.

*Enter King **CLAUDIUS** and two or three attendants*

CLAUDIUS
I have sent to seek him and to find the body.
How dangerous is it that this man goes loose!
Yet must not we put the strong law on him.
He's loved of the distracted multitude,
Who like not in their judgment, but their eyes.
And where 'tis so, th' offender's scourge is weighed,
But never the offense. To bear all smooth and even,
This sudden sending him away must seem
Deliberate pause. Diseases desperate grown
By desperate appliance are relieved,
Or not at all.

*Enter **ROSENCRANTZ***

How now, what hath befall'n?

ROSENCRANTZ
Where the dead body is bestowed, my lord,
We cannot get from him.

CLAUDIUS
But where is he?

ROSENCRANTZ
Without, my lord; guarded, to know your pleasure.

CLAUDIUS
Bring him before us.

ROSENCRANTZ
Ho, Guildenstern! Bring in my lord.

Enter **HAMLET** *and* **GUILDENSTERN**

CLAUDIUS
Now, Hamlet, where's Polonius?

HAMLET
At supper.

CLAUDIUS
At supper where?

HAMLET
Not where he eats, but where he is eaten. A certain convocation of politic worms are e'en at him. Your worm is your only emperor for diet. We fat all creatures else to fat us, and we fat ourselves for maggots. Your fat king and your lean beggar is but variable service—two dishes, but to one table. That's the end.

CLAUDIUS
Alas, alas!

HAMLET
A man may fish with the worm that hath eat of a king, and eat of the fish that hath fed of that worm.

CLAUDIUS
What dost you mean by this?

HAMLET
Nothing but to show you how a king may go a progress through the guts of a beggar.

CLAUDIUS
Where is Polonius?

HAMLET
In heaven. Send hither to see. If your messenger find him not there, seek him i' th' other place yourself. But if indeed you find him not within this month, you shall nose him as you go up the stairs into the lobby.

CLAUDIUS
(to attendants) Go seek him there.

Exeunt some attendants

HAMLET
He will stay till ye come.

CLAUDIUS
Hamlet, this deed, for thine especial safety—
Which we do tender as we dearly grieve
For that which thou hast done—must send thee hence
With fiery quickness. Therefore prepare thyself.
The bark is ready and the wind at help,
Th' associates tend, and everything is bent
For England.

HAMLET
For England?

CLAUDIUS
Ay, Hamlet.

HAMLET
Good.

CLAUDIUS
So is it, if thou knew'st our purposes.

HAMLET
I see a cherub that sees them. But come, for England.
Farewell, dear mother.

CLAUDIUS
Thy loving father, Hamlet.

HAMLET
My mother. Father and mother is man and wife, man and wife is
one flesh, and so, my mother.—Come, for England!

*Exit **HAMLET***

CLAUDIUS
Follow him at foot. Tempt him with speed aboard.
Delay it not. I'll have him hence tonight.
Away! For everything is sealed and done
That else leans on the affair. Pray you, make haste.

*Exeunt all but **CLAUDIUS***

And, England, if my love thou hold'st at aught—
As my great power thereof may give thee sense,

Since yet thy cicatrice looks raw and red
After the Danish sword and thy free awe
Pays homage to us—thou mayst not coldly set
Our sovereign process, which imports at full,
By letters congruing to that effect,
The present death of Hamlet. Do it, England,
For like the hectic in my blood he rages,
And thou must cure me. Till I know 'tis done,
Howe'er my haps, my joys were ne'er begun.

Exit

$\mathcal{A}$CT 4

$\mathcal{S}$cene 4

Hamlet encounters Fortinbras, a Norwegian prince leading an army into Poland to fight over a patch of land. Hamlet marvels that men will fight and kill over nothing, and yet he has failed to kill Claudius over a significant matter.

*Enter **FORTINBRAS** with his army and a **CAPTAIN***

FORTINBRAS

Go, Captain, from me greet the Danish king
Tell him that, by his license, Fortinbras
Craves the conveyance of a promised march
Over his kingdom. You know the rendezvous.
If that his majesty would aught with us,
We shall express our duty in his eye,
And let him know so.

CAPTAIN
I will do 't, my lord.

FORTINBRAS
Go softly on.

*Exeunt all except the **CAPTAIN***

*Enter **HAMLET, ROSENCRANTZ, GUILDENSTERN,** and others*

HAMLET
Good sir, whose powers are these?

CAPTAIN
They are of Norway, sir.

HAMLET
How purposed, sir, I pray you?

CAPTAIN
Against some part of Poland.

HAMLET
Who commands them, sir?

CAPTAIN
The nephew to old Norway, Fortinbras.

HAMLET
Goes it against the main of Poland, sir,
Or for some frontier?

CAPTAIN
Truly to speak, and with no addition,
We go to gain a little patch of ground
That hath in it no profit but the name.
To pay five ducats, five, I would not farm it.
Nor will it yield to Norway or the Pole
A ranker rate, should it be sold in fee.

HAMLET
Why, then the Polack never will defend it.

CAPTAIN

Yes, it is already garrisoned.

HAMLET

Two thousand souls and twenty thousand ducats
Will not debate the question of this straw.
This is th' impostume of much wealth and peace,
That inward breaks and shows no cause without
Why the man dies.—I humbly thank you, sir.

CAPTAIN

God be wi' you, sir.

*Exit **CAPTAIN***

ROSENCRANTZ

Will 't please you go, my lord?

HAMLET

I'll be with you straight. Go a little before.

*Exeunt all except **HAMLET***

How all occasions do inform against me,
And spur my dull revenge! What is a man
If his chief good and market of his time
Be but to sleep and feed? A beast, no more.
Sure, he that made us with such large discourse,
Looking before and after, gave us not
That capability and godlike reason
To fust in us unused. Now, whether it be
Bestial oblivion, or some craven scruple
Of thinking too precisely on th' event—

A thought which, quartered, hath but one part wisdom
And ever three parts coward—I do not know
Why yet I live to say "This thing's to do,"
Sith I have cause and will and strength and means
To do 't. Examples gross as earth exhort me.
Witness this army of such mass and charge
Led by a delicate and tender prince,
Whose spirit with divine ambition puffed
Makes mouths at the invisible event,
Exposing what is mortal and unsure
To all that fortune, death, and danger dare,
Even for an eggshell. Rightly to be great
Is not to stir without great argument,
But greatly to find quarrel in a straw
When honor's at the stake. How stand I then,
That have a father killed, a mother stained,
Excitements of my reason and my blood,
And let all sleep—while, to my shame, I see
The imminent death of twenty thousand men,
That for a fantasy and trick of fame
Go to their graves like beds, fight for a plot
Whereon the numbers cannot try the cause,
Which is not tomb enough and continent
To hide the slain? Oh, from this time forth,
My thoughts be bloody, or be nothing worth!

Exit

ACT 4

Scene 5

Ophelia goes mad over the death of Polonius, and Laertes returns from France, looking for revenge. Claudius convices Laertes to seek revenge on the right person.

*Enter **HORATIO, GERTRUDE**, and a **GENTLEMAN***

GERTRUDE
I will not speak with her.

GENTLEMAN
She is importunate,
Indeed distract. Her mood will needs be pitied.

GERTRUDE
What would she have?

GENTLEMAN
She speaks much of her father, says she hears
There's tricks i' th' world, and hems, and beats her heart,
Spurns enviously at straws, speaks things in doubt
That carry but half sense. Her speech is nothing,
Yet the unshaped use of it doth move
The hearers to collection. They aim at it,
And botch the words up fit to their own thoughts,
Which, as her winks and nods and gestures yield them,

Indeed would make one think there might be thought,
Though nothing sure, yet much unhappily.

HORATIO
'Twere good she were spoken with, for she may strew
Dangerous conjectures in ill-breeding minds.

GERTRUDE
Let her come in.

*Exit **GENTLEMAN***

(aside) To my sick soul (as sin's true nature is)
Each toy seems prologue to some great amiss.
So full of artless jealousy is guilt,
It spills itself in fearing to be spilt.

*Enter **OPHELIA**, distracted*

OPHELIA
Where is the beauteous majesty of Denmark?

GERTRUDE
How now, Ophelia?

OPHELIA
(sings)
How should I your true love know
From another one?
By his cockle hat and staff,
And his sandal shoon.

GERTRUDE
Alas, sweet lady, what imports this song?

OPHELIA

Say you? Nay, pray you, mark.
(sings)
He is dead and gone, lady,
He is dead and gone,
At his head a grass-green turf,
At his heels a stone.
Oh, ho!

GERTRUDE

Nay, but, Ophelia—

OPHELIA

Pray you, mark.
(sings)
White his shroud as the mountain snow—

Enter **CLAUDIUS**

GERTRUDE

Alas, look here, my lord.

Ophelia. [Sings.] Larded with sweet flowers;
Which bewept to the grave did go
With true-love showers.
Act IV. Scene V.

OPHELIA

(sings)
Larded all with sweet flowers,
Which bewept to the ground did not go
With true-love showers.

CLAUDIUS

How do you, pretty lady?

OPHELIA

Well, God'ield you! They say the owl was a baker's daughter. Lord, we know what we are, but know not what we may be. God be at your table.

CLAUDIUS

Conceit upon her father.

OPHELIA

Pray you, let's have no words of this, but when they ask you what it means, say you this:
(sings)
Tomorrow is Saint Valentine's day,
All in the morning betime,
And I a maid at your window,
To be your Valentine.
Then up he rose, and donned his clothes,
And dupped the chamber door.
Let in the maid that out a maid
Never departed more.

CLAUDIUS

Pretty Ophelia—

OPHELIA

Indeed, without an oath I'll make an end on 't:
(sings)
By Gis and by Saint Charity,
Alack, and fie, for shame!
Young men will do 't, if they come to 't.
By Cock, they are to blame.
Quoth she, "Before you tumbled me,
You promised me to wed."
He answers,
"So would I ha' done, by yonder sun,
An thou hadst not come to my bed."

CLAUDIUS

How long hath she been thus?

OPHELIA

I hope all will be well. We must be patient, but I cannot choose but weep, to think they should lay him i' th' cold ground. My brother shall know of it, and so I thank you for your good counsel. Come, my coach! Good night, ladies. Good night, sweet ladies. Good night, good night.

*Exit **OPHELIA***

CLAUDIUS

Follow her close. Give her good watch, I pray you.

*Exit **HORATIO***

Oh, this is the poison of deep grief. It springs
All from her father's death, and now behold!
O Gertrude, Gertrude,
When sorrows come, they come not single spies
But in battalions. First, her father slain.
Next, your son gone, and he most violent author
Of his own just remove. The people muddied,
Thick, and unwholesome in their thoughts and whispers
For good Polonius' death, and we have done but greenly
In hugger-mugger to inter him. Poor Ophelia
Divided from herself and her fair judgment,
Without the which we are pictures, or mere beasts.
Last—and as much containing as all these—
Her brother is in secret come from France,
Feeds on his wonder, keeps himself in clouds,
And wants not buzzers to infect his ear
With pestilent speeches of his father's death,
Wherein necessity, of matter beggared,

Will nothing stick our person to arraign
In ear and ear. O my dear Gertrude, this,
Like to a murdering piece, in many places
Gives me superfluous death.

A noise within

GERTRUDE
Alack, what noise is this?

CLAUDIUS
Where are my Switzers? Let them guard the door.

*Enter a **MESSENGER***

What is the matter?

MESSENGER
Save yourself, my lord.
The ocean, overpeering of his list,
Eats not the flats with more impiteous haste
Than young Laertes, in a riotous head,
O'erbears your officers. The rabble call him "lord"
And—as the world were now but to begin,
Antiquity forgot, custom not known,
The ratifiers and props of every word—
They cry, "Choose we! Laertes shall be king!"
Caps, hands, and tongues applaud it to the clouds:
"Laertes shall be king, Laertes king!"

GERTRUDE
How cheerfully on the false trail they cry.
O, this is counter, you false Danish dogs!

161

Noise within

CLAUDIUS
The doors are broke.

*Enter **LAERTES** with others*

LAERTES
Where is this king?—Sirs, stand you all without.

ALL
No, let's come in!

LAERTES
I pray you, give me leave.

ALL
We will, we will.

*Exeunt **LAERTES' FOLLOWERS***

LAERTES
I thank you. Keep the door.—O thou vile king,
Give me my father!

GERTRUDE
Calmly, good Laertes.

LAERTES
That drop of blood that's calm proclaims me bastard,
Cries "Cuckold!" to my father, brands the "harlot"
Even here between the chaste unsmirchèd brow
Of my true mother.

CLAUDIUS
What is the cause, Laertes,
That thy rebellion looks so giant-like?—
Let him go, Gertrude. Do not fear our person.
There's such divinity doth hedge a king
That treason can but peep to what it would,
Acts little of his will.—Tell me, Laertes,
Why thou art thus incensed.—Let him go, Gertrude.—
Speak, man.

LAERTES
Where is my father?

CLAUDIUS
Dead.

GERTRUDE
But not by him.

CLAUDIUS
Let him demand his fill.

LAERTES
How came he dead? I'll not be juggled with.
To hell, allegiance! Vows, to the blackest devil!
Conscience and grace, to the profoundest pit!
I dare damnation. To this point I stand
That both the worlds I give to negligence.
Let come what comes, only I'll be revenged
Most thoroughly for my father.

CLAUDIUS
Who shall stay you?

LAERTES
My will, not all the world.

And for my means, I'll husband them so well,
They shall go far with little.

CLAUDIUS
Good Laertes,
If you desire to know the certainty
Of your dear father's death, is 't writ in your revenge,
That, swoopstake, you will draw both friend and foe,
Winner and loser?

LAERTES
None but his enemies.

CLAUDIUS
Will you know them then?

LAERTES
To his good friends thus wide I'll ope my arms
And, like the kind life-rendering pelican,
Repast them with my blood.

CLAUDIUS
Why, now you speak
Like a good child and a true gentleman.
That I am guiltless of your father's death
And am most sensible in grief for it,
It shall as level to your judgment pierce
As day does to your eye.

Noise within: "Let her come in!"

LAERTES
How now? What noise is that?

164

*Enter **OPHELIA***

O heat, dry up my brains! Tears seven times salt,
Burn out the sense and virtue of mine eye!
By heaven, thy madness shall be paid by weight,
Till our scale turn the beam. O rose of May,
Dear maid, kind sister, sweet Ophelia!
O heavens, is 't possible a young maid's wits
Should be as mortal as an old man's life?
Nature is fine in love, and where 'tis fine,
It sends some precious instance of itself
After the thing it loves.

OPHELIA
(sings)
They bore him barefaced on the bier,
Hey, non nonny, nonny, hey, nonny,
And in his grave rained many a tear.
Fare you well, my dove.

LAERTES
Hadst thou thy wits, and didst persuade revenge,
It could not move thus.

OPHELIA
You must sing *A-down a-down*—And you, *Call him a- down-a—*
Oh, how the wheel becomes it! It is the false steward that stole his
master's daughter.

LAERTES
This nothing's more than matter.

OPHELIA
There's rosemary, that's for remembrance. Pray you, love,
remember. And there is pansies, that's for thoughts.

LAERTES

A document in madness. Thoughts and remembrance fitted.

OPHELIA

There's fennel for you, and columbines.—There's rue for you, and here's some for me. We may call it "herb of grace" o' Sundays.— Oh, you must wear your rue with a difference.—There's a daisy. I would give you some violets, but they withered all when my father died. They say he made a good end *(sings) For bonny sweet Robin is all my joy—*

LAERTES

Thought and affliction, passion, hell itself,
She turns to favor and to prettiness.

OPHELIA

(sings)
And will he not come again?
And will he not come again?
No, no, he is dead,
Go to thy deathbed.
He never will come again.
His beard was as white as snow,
All flaxen was his poll.
He is gone, he is gone,
And we cast away moan,
God ha' mercy on his soul.—
And of all Christian souls, I pray God. God be wi' ye.

*Exit **OPHELIA***

LAERTES

Do you see this, O God?

CLAUDIUS

Laertes, I must commune with your grief,
Or you deny me right. Go but apart,
Make choice of whom your wisest friends you will.
And they shall hear and judge 'twixt you and me.
If by direct or by collateral hand
They find us touched, we will our kingdom give,
Our crown, our life, and all that we can ours,
To you in satisfaction. But if not,
Be you content to lend your patience to us,
And we shall jointly labor with your soul
To give it due content.

LAERTES

Let this be so.
His means of death, his obscure funeral—
No trophy, sword, nor hatchment o'er his bones,
No noble rite nor formal ostentation—
Cry to be heard as 'twere from heaven to earth,
That I must call 't in question.

CLAUDIUS

So you shall.
And where the offense is, let the great ax fall.
I pray you, go with me.

Exeunt

ACT 4

Scene 6

Horatio receives a message that Hamlet's ship was attacked by pirates and that Hamlet has quietly returned to Denmark.

*Enter **HORATIO** and a **SERVANT***

HORATIO
What are they that would speak with me?

SERVANT
Seafaring men, sir. They say they have letters for you.

HORATIO
Let them come in.

*Exit **SERVANT***

I do not know from what part of the world
I should be greeted, if not from Lord Hamlet.

*Enter **SAILORS***

SAILOR
God bless you, sir.

HORATIO

Let him bless thee too.

SAILOR

He shall, sir, an 't please Him. There's a letter for you, sir— it comes from the ambassador that was bound for England—if your name be Horatio, as I am let to know it is. *(gives* HORATIO *a letter)*

HORATIO

(reads)

"Horatio,

When thou shalt have overlooked this, give these fellows some means to the king. They have letters for him. Ere we were two days old at sea, a pirate of very warlike appointment gave us chase. Finding ourselves too slow of sail, we put on a compelled valor, and in the grapple I boarded them. On the instant, they got clear of our ship, so I alone became their prisoner. They have dealt with me like thieves of mercy, but they knew what they did; I am to do a good turn for them.

Let the king have the letters I have sent, and repair thou to me with as much speed as thou wouldst fly death. I have words to speak in thine ear will make thee dumb, yet are they much too light for the bore of the matter. These good fellows will bring thee where I am. Rosencrantz and Guildenstern hold their course for England. Of them I have much to tell thee. Fare-well.

He that thou knowest thine, Hamlet."

Come, I will give you way for these your letters, And do 't the speedier, that you may direct me To him from whom you brought them.

Exeunt

ACT 4

Scene 7

Claudius and Laertes plot to kill Hamlet in a fencing contest. Laertes will fight with a poisoned sword, and Hamlet will be given a goblet of poison wine if he does well.

*Enter **CLAUDIUS** and **LAERTES***

CLAUDIUS
Now must your conscience my acquaintance seal,
And you must put me in your heart for friend,
Sith you have heard, and with a knowing ear,
That he which hath your noble father slain
Pursued my life.

LAERTES
It well appears. But tell me
Why you proceeded not against these feats,
So criminal and so capital in nature,
As by your safety, wisdom, all things else,
You mainly were stirred up.

CLAUDIUS
Oh, for two special reasons,
Which may to you perhaps seem much unsinewed,
But yet to me they are strong. The queen his mother
Lives almost by his looks, and for myself—

My virtue or my plague, be it either which—
She's so conjunctive to my life and soul,
That, as the star moves not but in his sphere,
I could not but by her. The other motive
Why to a public count I might not go,
Is the great love the general gender bear him,
Who, dipping all his faults in their affection,
Would, like the spring that turneth wood to stone,
Convert his gyves to graces—so that my arrows,
Too slightly timbered for so loud a wind,
Would have reverted to my bow again,
And not where I had aimed them.

LAERTES
And so have I a noble father lost,
A sister driven into desperate terms,
Whose worth, if praises may go back again,
Stood challenger on mount of all the age
For her perfections. But my revenge will come.

CLAUDIUS
Break not your sleeps for that. You must not think
That we are made of stuff so flat and dull
That we can let our beard be shook with danger
And think it pastime. You shortly shall hear more.
I loved your father, and we love ourself.
And that, I hope, will teach you to imagine—

*Enter a **MESSENGER***

How now, what news?

MESSENGER
Letters, my lord, from Hamlet.
This to your majesty, this to the queen. *(gives* CLAUDIUS *letters)*

CLAUDIUS

From Hamlet? Who brought them?

MESSENGER

Sailors, my lord, they say. I saw them not.
They were given me by Claudio. He received them
Of him that brought them.

CLAUDIUS

Laertes, you shall hear them.—Leave us.

Exit **MESSENGER**

(reads)
"High and mighty,
You shall know I am set naked on your kingdom. Tomorrow shall
I beg leave to see your kingly eyes, when I shall, first asking your
pardon thereunto, recount the occasion of my sudden and more
strange return.Hamlet."
What should this mean? Are all the rest come back? Or is it some
abuse, and no such thing?

LAERTES

Know you the hand?

CLAUDIUS

'Tis Hamlet's character. "Naked"?
And in a postscript here, he says "alone."
Can you advise me?

LAERTES

I'm lost in it, my lord. But let him come.
It warms the very sickness in my heart
That I shall live and tell him to his teeth,
"Thus diddest thou."

173

CLAUDIUS
If it be so, Laertes—
As how should it be so? How otherwise?—
Will you be ruled by me?

LAERTES
Ay, my lord—
So you will not o'errule me to a peace.

CLAUDIUS
To thine own peace. If he be now returned,
As checking at his voyage, and that he means
No more to undertake it, I will work him
To an exploit, now ripe in my devise,
Under the which he shall not choose but fall.
And for his death no wind of blame shall breathe,
But even his mother shall uncharge the practice
And call it accident.

LAERTES
My lord, I will be ruled
The rather if you could devise it so
That I might be the organ.

CLAUDIUS
It falls right.
You have been talked of since your travel much—
And that in Hamlet's hearing—for a quality
Wherein, they say, you shine. Your sum of parts
Did not together pluck such envy from him
As did that one, and that, in my regard,
Of the unworthiest siege.

LAERTES
What part is that, my lord?

CLAUDIUS
A very ribbon in the cap of youth,
Yet needful too, for youth no less becomes
The light and careless livery that it wears
Than settled age his sables and his weeds,
Importing health and graveness. Two months since,
Here was a gentleman of Normandy.
I've seen myself, and served against, the French,
And they can well on horseback. But this gallant
Had witchcraft in 't. He grew unto his seat,
And to such wondrous doing brought his horse
As he had been encorpsed and demi-natured
With the brave beast. So far he topped my thought,
That I, in forgery of shapes and tricks,
Come short of what he did.

LAERTES
A Norman was 't?

CLAUDIUS
A Norman.

LAERTES
Upon my life, Lamond!

CLAUDIUS
The very same.

LAERTES
I know him well. He is the brooch indeed
And gem of all the nation.

CLAUDIUS
He made confession of you,
And gave you such a masterly report

For art and exercise in your defense,
And for your rapier most especially,
That he cried out 'twould be a sight indeed
If one could match you. The 'scrimers of their nation,
He swore, had had neither motion, guard, nor eye,
If you opposed them. Sir, this report of his
Did Hamlet so envenom with his envy
That he could nothing do but wish and beg
Your sudden coming o'er, to play with him.
Now, out of this—

LAERTES
What out of this, my lord?

CLAUDIUS
Laertes, was your father dear to you?
Or are you like the painting of a sorrow,
A face without a heart?

LAERTES
Why ask you this?

CLAUDIUS
Not that I think you did not love your father
But that I know love is begun by time,
And that I see, in passages of proof,
Time qualifies the spark and fire of it.
There lives within the very flame of love
A kind of wick or snuff that will abate it.
And nothing is at a like goodness still.
For goodness, growing to a pleurisy,
Dies in his own too-much. That we would do,
We should do when we would, for this "would" changes
And hath abatements and delays as many
As there are tongues, are hands, are accidents.

176

And then this "should" is like a spendthrift sigh
That hurts by easing.—But to the quick of th' ulcer:
Hamlet comes back. What would you undertake
To show yourself in deed your father's son
More than in words?

LAERTES
To cut his throat i' th' church.

CLAUDIUS
No place, indeed, should murder sanctuarize.
Revenge should have no bounds. But, good Laertes,
Will you do this, keep close within your chamber.
Hamlet returned shall know you are come home.
We'll put on those shall praise your excellence
And set a double varnish on the fame
The Frenchman gave you, bring you in fine together
And wager on your heads. He, being remiss,
Most generous and free from all contriving,
Will not peruse the foils; so that, with ease,
Or with a little shuffling, you may choose
A sword unbated, and in a pass of practice
Requite him for your father.

King.   And, in a pass of practice,
Requite him for your father.
Laertes.   I will do 't;
And, for that purpose, I 'll anoint my sword.
Act IV. Scene VII.

LAERTES
I will do 't.
And for that purpose I'll anoint my sword.
I bought an unction of a mountebank,
So mortal that, but dip a knife in it,
Where it draws blood no cataplasm so rare,
Collected from all simples that have virtue
Under the moon, can save the thing from death
That is but scratched withal. I'll touch my point
With this contagion, that if I gall him slightly
It may be death.

CLAUDIUS
Let's further think of this,
Weigh what convenience both of time and means
May fit us to our shape. If this should fail,
And that our drift look through our bad performance,
'Twere better not assayed. Therefore this project
Should have a back or second that might hold
If this should blast in proof.—Soft, let me see.—
We'll make a solemn wager on your cunnings.—
I ha 't! When in your motion you are hot and dry,
As make your bouts more violent to that end,
And that he calls for drink, I'll have prepared him
A chalice for the nonce, whereon but sipping,
If he by chance escape your venomed stuck,
Our purpose may hold there.—But stay, what noise?

Enter **GERTRUDE**

GERTRUDE
One woe doth tread upon another's heel,
So fast they follow.—Your sister's drowned, Laertes.

LAERTES
Drowned? Oh, where?

GERTRUDE
There is a willow grows aslant a brook
That shows his hoar leaves in the glassy stream.
There with fantastic garlands did she come
Of crowflowers, nettles, daisies, and long purples,
That liberal shepherds give a grosser name,
But our cold maids do "dead men's fingers" call them.
There, on the pendant boughs her coronet weeds
Clambering to hang, an envious sliver broke,
When down her weedy trophies and herself

179

Fell in the weeping brook. Her clothes spread wide,
And mermaid-like a while they bore her up,
Which time she chanted snatches of old lauds
As one incapable of her own distress,
Or like a creature native and indued
Unto that element. But long it could not be
Till that her garments, heavy with their drink,
Pulled the poor wretch from her melodious lay
To muddy death.

LAERTES
Alas, then she is drowned.

GERTRUDE
Drowned, drowned.

LAERTES
Too much of water hast thou, poor Ophelia,
And therefore I forbid my tears. But yet
It is our trick. Nature her custom holds,
Let shame say what it will. When these are gone,
The woman will be out.—Adieu, my lord.
I have a speech of fire that fain would blaze,
But that this folly doubts it.

*Exit **LAERTES***

CLAUDIUS
Let's follow, Gertrude.
How much I had to do to calm his rage!
Now fear I this will give it start again.
Therefore let's follow.

Exeunt

ACT 5

Scene 1

Hamlet and Horatio wait in a graveyard when Ophelia's funeral procession arrives. Hamlet and Laertes fight in Ophelia's grave until they are pulled apart.

*Enter a **GRAVEDIGGER** and the **OTHER** gravedigger*

GRAVEDIGGER
Is she to be buried in Christian burial when she willfully seeks her own salvation?

OTHER
I tell thee she is. Therefore make her grave straight. The crowner hath sat on her and finds it Christian burial.

GRAVEDIGGER
How can that be, unless she drowned herself in her own defense?

OTHER
Why, 'tis found so.

GRAVEDIGGER
It must be *se offendendo*. It cannot be else. For here lies the point: if I drown myself wittingly, it argues an act. And an act hath three branches—it is to act, to do, to perform. Argal, she drowned herself wittingly.

181

OTHER

Nay, but hear you, Goodman Delver—

GRAVEDIGGER

Give me leave. Here lies the water. Good. Here stands the man. Good. If the man go to this water and drown himself, it is, will he nill he, he goes. Mark you that. But if the water come to him and drown him, he drowns not himself. Argal, he that is not guilty of his own death shortens not his own life.

OTHER

But is this law?

GRAVEDIGGER

Ay, marry, is 't. Crowner's quest law.

OTHER

Will you ha' the truth on 't? If this had not been a gentlewoman, she should have been buried out o' Christian burial.

GRAVEDIGGER

Why, there thou sayst. And the more pity that great folk should have countenance in this world to drown or hang themselves more than their even Christian. Come, my spade. There is no ancient gentleman but gardeners, ditchers, and grave-makers. They hold up Adam's profession.

OTHER

Was he a gentleman?

GRAVEDIGGER

He was the first that ever bore arms.

OTHER

Why, he had none.

GRAVEDIGGER

What, art a heathen? How dost thou understand the Scripture? The Scripture says Adam digged. Could he dig without arms? I'll put another question to thee. If thou answerest me not to the purpose, confess thyself—

OTHER

Go to.

GRAVEDIGGER

What is he that builds stronger than either the mason, the shipwright, or the carpenter?

OTHER

The gallows-maker, for that frame outlives a thousand tenants.

GRAVEDIGGER

I like thy wit well, in good faith. The gallows does well, but how does it well? It does well to those that do ill.

Now thou dost ill to say the gallows is built stronger than the church. Argal, the gallows may do well to thee. To 't again, come.

OTHER

"Who builds stronger than a mason, a shipwright, or a carpenter?"

GRAVEDIGGER

Ay, tell me that, and unyoke.

OTHER

Marry, now I can tell.

GRAVEDIGGER

To 't.

OTHER

Mass, I cannot tell.

*Enter **HAMLET** and **HORATIO** afar off*

GRAVEDIGGER

Cudgel thy brains no more about it, for your dull ass will not mend his pace with beating. And when you are asked this question next, say "A grave-maker." The houses that he makes last till doomsday. Go, get thee in. Fetch me a stoup of liquor.

*Exit **OTHER***

(digs and sings)
In youth when I did love, did love,
Methought it was very sweet
To contract—o—the time, for—a—my behove,
Oh, methought, there—a—was nothing—a—meet.

HAMLET

Has this fellow no feeling of his business? He sings at grave-making.

HORATIO

Custom hath made it in him a property of easiness.

HAMLET

'Tis e'en so. The hand of little employment hath the daintier sense.

GRAVEDIGGER

(sings)
But age with his stealing steps

184

Hath clawed me in his clutch,
And hath shipped me into the land
As if I had never been such.
(throws up a skull)

HAMLET

That skull had a tongue in it and could sing once. How the knave jowls it to the ground, as if it were Cain's jawbone, that did the first murder! It might be the pate of a politician, which this ass now o'erreaches, one that would circumvent God, might it not?

HORATIO

It might, my lord.

HAMLET

Or of a courtier, which could say, "Good morrow, sweet lord!" "How dost thou, good lord?" This might be my Lord Such-a-one that praised my Lord Such-a-one's horse when he meant to beg it, might it not?

HORATIO

Ay, my lord.

HAMLET

Why, e'en so. And now my Lady Worm's, chapless and knocked about the mazard with a sexton's spade. Here's fine revolution, an we had the trick to see 't. Did these bones cost no more the breeding but to play at loggets with them? Mine ache to think on 't.

GRAVEDIGGER

(sings)
A pickax and a spade, a spade,
For and a shrouding sheet,
Oh, a pit of clay for to be made

For such a guest is meet.
(throws up another skull)

HAMLET
There's another. Why may not that be the skull of a lawyer? Where be his quiddities now, his quillities, his cases, his tenures, and his tricks? Why does he suffer this rude knave now to knock him about the sconce with a dirty shovel and will not tell him of his action of battery? Hum! This fellow might be in 's time a great buyer of land, with his statutes, his recognizances, his fines, his double vouchers, his recoveries. Is this the fine of his fines and the recovery of his recoveries, to have his fine pate full of fine dirt? Will his vouchers vouch him no more of his purchases, and double ones too, than the length and breadth of a pair of indentures? The very conveyances of his lands will hardly lie in this box, and must the inheritor himself have no more, ha?

HORATIO
Not a jot more, my lord.

HAMLET
Is not parchment made of sheepskins?

HORATIO
Ay, my lord, and of calfskins too.

HAMLET
They are sheep and calves which seek out assurance in that. I will speak to this fellow.—Whose grave's this, sirrah?

GRAVEDIGGER
Mine, sir.
(sings)
Oh, a pit of clay for to be made
For such a guest is meet.

186

HAMLET

I think it be thine, indeed, for thou liest in 't.

GRAVEDIGGER

You lie out on 't, sir, and therefore it is not yours. For my part, I do not lie in 't, and yet it is mine.

HAMLET

Thou dost lie in 't, to be in 't and say it is thine. 'Tis for the dead, not for the quick. Therefore thou liest.

GRAVEDIGGER

'Tis a quick lie, sir. 'Twill away gain from me to you.

HAMLET

What man dost thou dig it for?

GRAVEDIGGER

For no man, sir.

HAMLET

What woman, then?

GRAVEDIGGER

For none, neither.

HAMLET

Who is to be buried in 't?

GRAVEDIGGER

One that was a woman, sir, but, rest her soul, she's dead.

HAMLET

How absolute the knave is! We must speak by the card, or equivocation will undo us. By the Lord, Horatio, these three years I have taken a note of it. The age is grown so picked that the toe of the peasant comes so near the heel of the courtier he galls his kibe.—How long hast thou been a grave-maker?

GRAVEDIGGER
Of all the days i' the year, I came to 't that day that our last King Hamlet overcame Fortinbras.

HAMLET
How long is that since?

GRAVEDIGGER
Cannot you tell that? Every fool can tell that. It was the very day that young Hamlet was born, he that is mad and sent into England.

HAMLET
Ay, marry, why was he sent into England?

GRAVEDIGGER
Why, because he was mad. He shall recover his wits there, or, if he do not, it's no great matter there.

HAMLET
Why?

GRAVEDIGGER
'Twill not be seen in him there. There the men are as mad as he.

HAMLET
How came he mad?

GRAVEDIGGER
Very strangely, they say.

HAMLET
How "strangely"?

GRAVEDIGGER

Faith, e'en with losing his wits.

HAMLET

Upon what ground?

GRAVEDIGGER

Why, here in Denmark. I have been sexton here, man and boy, thirty years.

HAMLET

How long will a man lie i' the earth ere he rot?

GRAVEDIGGER

Faith, if he be not rotten before he die—as we have many pocky corses nowadays that will scarce hold the laying in— he will last you some eight year or nine year. A tanner will last you nine year.

HAMLET

Why he more than another?

GRAVEDIGGER

Why, sir, his hide is so tanned with his trade that he will keep out water a great while, and your water is a sore decayer of your whoreson dead body. *(indicates a skull)* Here's a skull now. This skull has lain in the earth three-and-twenty years.

HAMLET

Whose was it?

GRAVEDIGGER

A whoreson mad fellow's it was. Whose do you think it was?

HAMLET

Nay, I know not.

GRAVEDIGGER

A pestilence on him for a mad rogue! He poured a flagon of Rhenish on my head once. This same skull, sir, was Yorick's skull, the king's jester.

HAMLET

This?

GRAVEDIGGER

E'en that.

HAMLET

Let me see. *(takes the skull)* Alas, poor Yorick! I knew him, Horatio, a fellow of infinite jest, of most excellent fancy. He hath borne me on his back a thousand times, and now, how abhorred in my imagination it is! My gorge rises at it. Here hung those lips that I have kissed I know not how oft. —Where be your gibes now? Your gambols? Your songs? Your flashes of merriment that were wont to set the table on a roar? Not one now to mock your own grinning? Quite chapfallen? Now get you to my lady's chamber and tell her, let her paint an inch thick, to this favor she must come. Make her laugh at that.—Prithee, Horatio, tell me one thing.

First Clown. This same skull, sir, was Yorick's skull, the king's jester.
Hamlet. This?
First Clown. E'en that.
Hamlet. Let me see.   *Act V. Scene I*

HORATIO
What's that, my lord?

HAMLET
Dost thou think Alexander looked o' this fashion i' th' earth?

HORATIO
E'en so.

HAMLET
And smelt so? Pah! *(puts down the skull)*

HORATIO

E'en so, my lord.

HAMLET

Alexander till he find it stopping a bunghole?

HORATIO

'Twere to consider too curiously, to consider so.

HAMLET

No, faith, not a jot. But to follow him thither with modesty enough, and likelihood to lead it, as thus: Alexander died, Alexander was buried, Alexander returneth to dust, the dust is earth, of earth we make loam—and why of that loam, whereto he was converted, might they not stop a beer barrel?
Imperious Caesar, dead and turned to clay,
Might stop a hole to keep the wind away.
Oh, that that earth, which kept the world in awe,
Should patch a wall t' expel the winter's flaw!
But soft, but soft a while.

Enter King **CLAUDIUS**, *Queen* **GERTRUDE**, **LAERTES**, *and a coffin, with a* **PRIEST** *and other lords attendant.*

Here comes the king,
The queen, the courtiers—who is this they follow,
And with such maimèd rites? This doth betoken
The corse they follow did with desperate hand
Fordo its own life. 'Twas of some estate.
Couch we a while and mark.

HAMLET *and* **HORATIO** *withdraw*

LAERTES

What ceremony else?

192

HAMLET
That is Laertes, a very noble youth, mark.

LAERTES
What ceremony else?

PRIEST
Her obsequies have been as far enlarged
As we have warranty. Her death was doubtful,
And, but that great command o'ersways the order,
She should in ground unsanctified have lodged
Till the last trumpet. For charitable prayers
Shards, flints and pebbles should be thrown on her.
Yet here she is allowed her virgin crants,
Her maiden strewments, and the bringing home
Of bell and burial.

LAERTES
Must there no more be done?

PRIEST
No more be done.
We should profane the service of the dead
To sing a requiem and such rest to her
As to peace-parted souls.

LAERTES
Lay her i' th' earth,
And from her fair and unpolluted flesh
May violets spring! I tell thee, churlish priest,
A ministering angel shall my sister be
When thou liest howling.

HAMLET
(to HORATIO*)* What, the fair Ophelia?

GERTRUDE

Sweets to the sweet. Farewell! *(scatters flowers)*
I hoped thou shouldst have been my Hamlet's wife.
I thought thy bride-bed to have decked, sweet maid,
And not have strewed thy grave.

LAERTES

Oh, treble woe
Fall ten times treble on that cursèd head,
Whose wicked deed thy most ingenious sense
Deprived thee of! Hold off the earth awhile
Till I have caught her once more in mine arms.
(leaps into the grave)
Now pile your dust upon the quick and dead,
Till of this flat a mountain you have made,
T' o'ertop old Pelion or the skyish head
Of blue Olympus.

HAMLET

(comes forward) What is he whose grief
Bears such an emphasis, whose phrase of sorrow
Conjures the wandering stars, and makes them stand
Like wonder-wounded hearers? This is I,
Hamlet the Dane. *(leaps into the grave)*

LAERTES

The devil take thy soul!

HAMLET *and* **LAERTES** *grapple*

HAMLET

Thou pray'st not well.
I prithee, take thy fingers from my throat,

For though I am not splenitive and rash,
Yet have I something in me dangerous,
Which let thy wisdom fear. Hold off thy hand.

CLAUDIUS
Pluck them asunder.

GERTRUDE
Hamlet, Hamlet!

ALL
Gentlemen—

HORATIO
(to HAMLET*)* Good my lord, be quiet.

*Attendants separate **HAMLET** and **LAERTES***

HAMLET
Why, I will fight with him upon this theme
Until my eyelids will no longer wag.

GERTRUDE
O my son, what theme?

HAMLET
I loved Ophelia. Forty thousand brothers
Could not with all their quantity of love
Make up my sum. What wilt thou do for her?

CLAUDIUS
O, he is mad, Laertes.

GERTRUDE
For love of God, forbear him.

195

HAMLET

'Swounds, show me what thou'lt do.

Woo't weep? Woo't fight? Woo't fast? Woo't tear thyself?

Woo't drink up eisel, eat a crocodile?

I'll do 't. Dost thou come here to whine,

To outface me with leaping in her grave?

Be buried quick with her?—and so will I.

And if thou prate of mountains let them throw

Millions of acres on us, till our ground,

Singeing his pate against the burning zone,

Make Ossa like a wart! Nay, an thou'lt mouth,

I'll rant as well as thou.

GERTRUDE

This is mere madness.

And thus a while the fit will work on him.

Anon, as patient as the female dove

When that her golden couplets are disclosed,

His silence will sit drooping.

HAMLET

Hear you, sir.

What is the reason that you use me thus?

I loved you ever. But it is no matter.

Let Hercules himself do what he may,

The cat will mew and dog will have his day.

Exit **HAMLET**

CLAUDIUS

I pray thee, good Horatio, wait upon him.

*Exit **HORATIO***

(to LAERTES*)* Strengthen your patience in our last night's speech.
We'll put the matter to the present push.—
Good Gertrude, set some watch over your son.—
This grave shall have a living monument.
An hour of quiet shortly shall we see.
Till then in patience our proceeding be.

Exeunt

ACT 5

Scene 2

Hamlet and Laertes duel. Laertes dies by his own poisoned sword. Gertrude dies after drinking the poisoned cup. Claudius dies by Hamlet's sword and then poison. Hamlet dies by the poison from Laertes's sword. Prince Fortinbras orders Hamlet to be buried with honor.

*Enter **HAMLET** and **HORATIO***

HAMLET
So much for this, sir. Now shall you see the other.
You do remember all the circumstance?

HORATIO
Remember it, my lord?

HAMLET
Sir, in my heart there was a kind of fighting
That would not let me sleep. Methought I lay
Worse than the mutines in the bilboes. Rashly—
And praised be rashness for it: let us know
Our indiscretion sometimes serves us well
When our deep plots do pall, and that should teach us
There's a divinity that shapes our ends,
Rough-hew them how we will—

HORATIO
That is most certain.

HAMLET
Up from my cabin,
My sea-gown scarfed about me, in the dark
Groped I to find out them, had my desire,
Fingered their packet, and in fine withdrew
To mine own room again, making so bold
(My fears forgetting manners) to unseal
Their grand commission, where I found, Horatio—
O royal knavery!—an exact command,
Larded with many several sorts of reasons
Importing Denmark's health, and England's too,
With—ho!—such bugs and goblins in my life
That, on the supervise (no leisure bated,
No, not to stay the grinding of the ax)
My head should be struck off.

HORATIO
Is 't possible?

HAMLET
(shows HORATIO *a document)*
Here's the commission. Read it at more leisure.
But wilt thou hear me how I did proceed?

HORATIO
I beseech you.

HAMLET
Being thus benetted round with villainies—
Ere I could make a prologue to my brains,
They had begun the play—I sat me down,
Devised a new commission, wrote it fair.
I once did hold it, as our statists do,
A baseness to write fair, and labored much

How to forget that learning, but, sir, now
It did me yeoman's service. Wilt thou know
Th' effect of what I wrote?

HORATIO
Ay, good my lord.

HAMLET
An earnest conjuration from the king,
As England was his faithful tributary,
As love between them like the palm might flourish,
As peace should stiff her wheaten garland wear
And stand a comma 'tween their amities,
And many suchlike "as's" of great charge,
That, on the view and knowing of these contents,
Without debatement further, more or less,
He should the bearers put to sudden death,
Not shriving time allowed.

HORATIO
How was this sealed?

HAMLET
Why, even in that was heaven ordinant.
I had my father's signet in my purse,
Which was the model of that Danish seal.
Folded the writ up in form of th' other,
Subscribed it, gave 't th' impression, placed it safely,
The changeling never known. Now, the next day
Was our sea fight, and what to this was sequent
Thou know'st already.

HORATIO
So Guildenstern and Rosencrantz go to 't.

HAMLET

Why, man, they did make love to this employment.
They are not near my conscience. Their defeat
Does by their own insinuation grow.
'Tis dangerous when the baser nature comes
Between the pass and fell incensèd points
Of mighty opposites.

HORATIO

Why, what a king is this!

HAMLET

Does it not, think thee, stand me now upon—
He that hath killed my king and whored my mother,
Popped in between th' election and my hopes,
Thrown out his angle for my proper life
(And with such cozenage!)—is 't not perfect conscience
To quit him with this arm? And is 't not to be damned
To let this canker of our nature come
In further evil?

HORATIO

It must be shortly known to him from England
What is the issue of the business there.

HAMLET

It will be short. The interim's mine.
And a man's life's no more than to say "one."
But I am very sorry, good Horatio,
That to Laertes I forgot myself,
For by the image of my cause I see
The portraiture of his. I'll court his favors.
But sure the bravery of his grief did put me
Into a towering passion.

HORATIO

Peace.—Who comes here?

*Enter young **OSRIC**, a courtier, hat in hand*

OSRIC

Your lordship is right welcome back to Denmark.

HAMLET

I humbly thank you, sir. *(aside to* HORATIO*)* Dost know this water-fly?

HORATIO

(aside to HAMLET*)* No, my good lord.

HAMLET

(aside to HORATIO*)* Thy state is the more gracious, for 'tis a vice to know him. He hath much land, and fertile. Let a beast be lord of beasts and his crib shall stand at the king's mess. 'Tis a chough, but, as I say, spacious in the possession of dirt.

OSRIC

Sweet lord, if your lordship were at leisure, I should impart a thing to you from His Majesty.

HAMLET

I will receive it, sir, with all diligence of spirit. Put your bonnet to his right use. 'Tis for the head.

OSRIC

I thank your lordship. It is very hot.

HAMLET

No, believe me, 'tis very cold. The wind is northerly.

OSRIC

It is indifferent cold, my lord, indeed.

HAMLET

But yet methinks it is very sultry and hot for my complexion.

OSRIC

Exceedingly, my lord. It is very sultry—as 'twere—I cannot tell how. My lord, his majesty bade me signify to you that he has laid a great wager on your head. Sir, this is the matter—

HAMLET

I beseech you, remember—*(indicates that* OSRIC *should put on his hat)*

OSRIC

Nay, good my lord, for mine ease, in good faith. Sir, here is newly come to court Laertes, believe me, an absolute gentleman, full of most excellent differences, of very soft society and great showing. Indeed, to speak feelingly of him, he is the card or calendar of gentry, for you shall find in him the continent of what part a gentleman would see.

HAMLET

Sir, his definement suffers no perdition in you, though I know to divide him inventorially would dizzy th' arithmetic of memory, and yet but yaw neither, in respect of his quick sail.

But in the verity of extolment, I take him to be a soul of great article, and his infusion of such dearth and rareness as, to make true diction of him, his semblable is his mirror. And who else would trace him? His umbrage, nothing more.

OSRIC

Your lordship speaks most infallibly of him.

HAMLET

The concernancy, sir? Why do we wrap the gentleman in our more rawer breath?

OSRIC

Sir?

HORATIO

(aside to HAMLET*)* Is 't not possible to understand in another tongue? You will do 't, sir, really.

HAMLET

What imports the nomination of this gentleman?

OSRIC

Of Laertes?

HORATIO

(aside to HAMLET*)* His purse is empty already. All 's golden words are spent.

HAMLET

Of him, sir.

OSRIC

I know you are not ignorant—

HAMLET

I would you did, sir. Yet in faith, if you did, it would not much approve me. Well, sir?

OSRIC

You are not ignorant of what excellence Laertes is—

HAMLET

I dare not confess that lest I should compare with him in excellence, but to know a man well were to know himself.

OSRIC

I mean, sir, for his weapon. But in the imputation laid on him by them, in his meed he's unfellowed.

HAMLET

What's his weapon?

OSRIC

Rapier and dagger.

HAMLET

That's two of his weapons. But well.

OSRIC

The king, sir, hath wagered with him six Barbary horses, against the which he has impawned, as I take it, six French rapiers and poniards with their assigns—as girdle, hangers, and so. Three of the carriages, in faith, are very dear to fancy, very responsive to the hilts, most delicate carriages, and of very liberal conceit.

HAMLET

What call you the carriages?

HORATIO

(aside to HAMLET*)* I knew you must be edified by the margin ere you had done.

OSRIC

The carriages, sir, are the hangers.

HAMLET

The phrase would be more germane to the matter if we could carry cannon by our sides. I would it might be hangers till then. But, on: six Barbary horses against six French swords, their assigns, and three liberal-conceited carriages—that's the French bet against the Danish. Why is this "impawned," as you call it?

OSRIC

The king, sir, hath laid that in a dozen passes between yourself and him, he shall not exceed you three hits. He hath laid on twelve for nine, and it would come to immediate trial if your lordship would vouchsafe the answer.

HAMLET

How if I answer "No"?

OSRIC

I mean, my lord, the opposition of your person in trial.

HAMLET

Sir, I will walk here in the hall. If it please His Majesty, 'tis the breathing time of day with me. Let the foils be brought, the gentleman willing, and the king hold his purpose. I will win for him an I can. If not, I will gain nothing but my shame and the odd hits.

OSRIC

Shall I redeliver you e'en so?

HAMLET

To this effect, sir, after what flourish your nature will.

OSRIC

I commend my duty to your lordship.

HAMLET

Yours, yours.

*Exit **OSRIC***

He does well to commend it himself. There are no tongues else for 's turn.

HORATIO

This lapwing runs away with the shell on his head.

HAMLET

He did comply, sir, with his dug before he sucked it. Thus has he—and many more of the same bevy that I know the drossy age dotes on—only got the tune of the time and outward habit of encounter, a kind of yeasty collection, which carries them through and through the most fond and winnowed opinions; and do but blow them to their trial, the bubbles are out.

Enter a **LORD**

LORD

My lord, his majesty commended him to you by young Osric, who brings back to him that you attend him in the hall. He sends to know if your pleasure hold to play with Laertes, or that you will take longer time.

HAMLET

I am constant to my purpose. They follow the king's pleasure. If his fitness speaks, mine is ready, now or whensoever, provided I be so able as now.

LORD

The king and queen and all are coming down.

HAMLET

In happy time.

LORD

The queen desires you to use some gentle entertainment to Laertes before you fall to play.

*Exit **LORD***

HAMLET
She well instructs me.

HORATIO
You will lose this wager, my lord.

HAMLET
I do not think so. Since he went into France, I have been in continual practice. I shall win at the odds. But thou wouldst not think how ill all's here about my heart. But it is no matter.

HORATIO
Nay, good my lord—

HAMLET
It is but foolery, but it is such a kind of gain-giving as would perhaps trouble a woman.

HORATIO
If your mind dislike anything, obey it. I will forestall their repair hither and say you are not fit.

HAMLET
Not a whit. We defy augury. There's a special providence in the fall of a sparrow. If it be now, 'tis not to come. If it be not to come, it will be now. If it be not now, yet it will come—the readiness is all. Since no man of aught e leaves knows, what is 't to leave betimes? Let be.

*Enter King **CLAUDIUS**, Queen **GERTRUDE, LAERTES, OSRIC**, lords, and other attendants with trumpets, drums, foils, a table, and flagons of wine*

CLAUDIUS
Come, Hamlet, come, and take this hand from me. *(puts LAERTES› hand into HAMLET›s)*

HAMLET
Give me your pardon, sir. I've done you wrong.
But pardon 't, as you are a gentleman.
This presence knows,
And you must needs have heard, how I am punished
With sore distraction. What I have done,
That might your nature, honor, and exception
Roughly awake, I here proclaim was madness.
Was 't Hamlet wronged Laertes? Never Hamlet.
If Hamlet from himself be ta'en away,
And when he's not himself does wrong Laertes,
Then Hamlet does it not. Hamlet denies it.
Who does it, then? His madness. If 't be so,
Hamlet is of the faction that is wronged.
His madness is poor Hamlet's enemy.
Sir, in this audience,
Let my disclaiming from a purposed evil
Free me so far in your most generous thoughts
That I have shot mine arrow o'er the house
And hurt my brother.

LAERTES
I am satisfied in nature,
Whose motive in this case should stir me most
To my revenge. But in my terms of honor
I stand aloof, and will no reconcilement
Till by some elder masters, of known honor,
I have a voice and precedent of peace
To keep my name ungored. But till that time
I do receive your offered love like love
And will not wrong it.

HAMLET

I embrace it freely,
And will this brother's wager frankly play.—
Give us the foils. Come on.

LAERTES

Come, one for me.

HAMLET

I'll be your foil, Laertes. In mine ignorance
Your skill shall, like a star i' th' darkest night,
Stick fiery off indeed.

LAERTES

You mock me, sir.

HAMLET

No, by this hand.

CLAUDIUS

Give them the foils, young Osric.—Cousin Hamlet,
You know the wager?

HAMLET

Very well, my lord.
Your grace hath laid the odds o' th' weaker side.

CLAUDIUS

I do not fear it. I have seen you both.
But since he is better we have therefore odds.

LAERTES

(tests a rapier) This is too heavy. Let me see another.

HAMLET

(tests a rapier) This likes me well. These foils have all a length?

211

OSRIC
Ay, my good lord.

HAMLET and LAERTES prepare to play

CLAUDIUS
Set me the stoups of wine upon that table.
If Hamlet give the first or second hit
Or quit in answer of the third exchange,
Let all the battlements their ordnance fire!
The king shall drink to Hamlet's better breath,
And in the cup an union shall he throw
Richer than that which four successive kings
In Denmark's crown have worn. Give me the cups.
And let the kettle to the trumpet speak,
The trumpet to the cannoneer without,
The cannons to the heavens, the heavens to earth,
"Now the king dunks to Hamlet." Come, begin.—
And you, the judges, bear a wary eye.

Trumpets

HAMLET
Come on, sir.

LAERTES
Come, my lord.

HAMLET and LAERTES play

HAMLET
One.

LAERTES

No.

HAMLET

Judgment?

OSRIC

A hit, a very palpable hit.

LAERTES

Well, again.

CLAUDIUS

Stay, give me drink.—Hamlet, this pearl is thine.
Here's to thy health.

Drums, trumpets sound, shot goes off

CLAUDIUS *drops pearl into cup*

Give him the cup.

HAMLET

I'll play this bout first. Set it by a while.
Come.

HAMLET *and* ***LAERTES*** *play*

Another hit. What say you?

LAERTES

A touch, a touch, I do confess 't.

CLAUDIUS

Our son shall win.

213

GERTRUDE
He's fat, and scant of breath.—
Here, Hamlet, take my napkin, rub thy brows.
The queen carouses to thy fortune, Hamlet.
(picks up the cup with the pearl)

HAMLET
Good madam.

CLAUDIUS
Gertrude, do not drink.

GERTRUDE
I will, my lord. I pray you, pardon me. *(drinks)*

CLAUDIUS
(aside) It is the poisoned cup. It is too late.

HAMLET
I dare not drink yet, madam. By and by.

GERTRUDE
Come, let me wipe thy face.

LAERTES
(aside to CLAUDIUS*)* My lord, I'll hit him now.

CLAUDIUS
I do not think 't.

LAERTES
(aside) And yet it is almost 'gainst my conscience.

HAMLET
Come, for the third, Laertes. You do but dally.
I pray you, pass with your best violence.
I am afeard you make a wanton of me.

214

LAERTES

Say you so? Come on.

HAMLET and LAERTES play

OSRIC

Nothing, neither way.

LAERTES

Have at you now!

LAERTES wounds HAMLET In scuffling, they change rapiers.
HAMLET wounds LAERTES

CLAUDIUS

Part them! They are incensed.

HAMLET

Nay, come, again.

GERTRUDE falls

OSRIC

Look to the queen there, ho!

HORATIO

They bleed on both sides.—How is it, my lord?

OSRIC

How is 't, Laertes?

LAERTES

Why, as a woodcock to mine own springe, Osric. I am justly killed with mine own treachery. *(falls)*

HAMLET
How does the queen?

CLAUDIUS
She swoons to see them bleed.

GERTRUDE
No, no, the drink, the drink!—O my dear Hamlet!
The drink, the drink! I am poisoned. *(dies)*

HAMLET
O villainy! Ho, let the door be locked.

*Exit **OSRIC***

Treachery! Seek it out.

LAERTES
It is here, Hamlet. Hamlet, thou art slain.
No medicine in the world can do thee good.
In thee there is not half an hour of life.
The treacherous instrument is in thy hand,
Unbated and envenomed. The foul practice
Hath turned itself on me. Lo, here I lie,
Never to rise again. Thy mother's poisoned.
I can no more. The king, the king's to blame.

HAMLET
The point envenomed too!—Then, venom, to thy work.

HAMLET** hurts **CLAUDIUS

ALL
Treason! Treason!

216

CLAUDIUS

O, yet defend me, friends. I am but hurt.

HAMLET

Here, thou incestuous, murderous, damnèd Dane,
Drink off this potion. Is thy union here?
Follow my mother.

*HAMLET forces **CLAUDIUS** to drink* ***CLAUDIUS*** *dies*

LAERTES

He is justly served.
It is a poison tempered by himself.
Exchange forgiveness with me, noble Hamlet.
Mine and my father's death come not upon thee,
Nor thine on me. *(dies)*

HAMLET

Heaven make thee free of it. I follow thee.—
I am dead, Horatio.—Wretched queen, adieu!—
You that look pale and tremble at this chance,
That are but mutes or audience to this act,
Had I but time (as this fell sergeant, Death,
Is strict in his arrest), O, I could tell you—
But let it be.—Horatio, I am dead.
Thou livest. Report me and my cause aright
To the unsatisfied.

HORATIO

Never believe it.
I am more an antique Roman than a Dane.
Here's yet some liquor left.
(lifts the poisoned cup)

HAMLET
As thou'rt a man,
Give me the cup. Let go! By heaven, I'll have 't.
(takes cup from HORATIO*)*
O God, Horatio, what a wounded name,
Things standing thus unknown, shall live behind me!
If thou didst ever hold me in thy heart
Absent thee from felicity a while,
And in this harsh world draw thy breath in pain
To tell my story.
March afar off and shout within
What warlike noise is this?

Enter **OSRIC**

OSRIC
Young Fortinbras, with conquest come from Poland,
To th' ambassadors of England gives
This warlike volley.

HAMLET
O, I die, Horatio.
The potent poison quite o'ercrows my spirit.
I cannot live to hear the news from England.
But I do prophesy the election lights
On Fortinbras. He has my dying voice.
So tell him, with th' occurrents, more and less,
Which have solicited. The rest is silence.
O, O, O, O. *(dies)*

HORATIO
Now cracks a noble heart.—Good night, sweet prince,
And flights of angels sing thee to thy rest!—
Why does the drum come hither?

Horatio. Now cracks a noble heart; good night, sweet prince:
And flights of angels sing thee to thy rest! *Act V. Scene II.*

*Enter **FORTINBRAS** and the English **AMBASSADOR**, with drummer and attendants*

FORTINBRAS
Where is this sight?

HORATIO
What is it ye would see?
If aught of woe or wonder, cease your search.

219

FORTINBRAS

This quarry cries on havoc. O proud death,
What feast is toward in thine eternal cell,
That thou so many princes at a shot
So bloodily hast struck?

AMBASSADOR

The sight is dismal,
And our affairs from England come too late.
The ears are senseless that should give us hearing,
To tell him his commandment is fulfilled,
That Rosencrantz and Guildenstern are dead.
Where should we have our thanks?

HORATIO

(*indicates* CLAUDIUS)   Not from his mouth,
Had it th' ability of life to thank you.
He never gave commandment for their death.
But since so jump upon this bloody question,
You from the Polack wars, and you from England,
Are here arrived, give order that these bodies
High on a stage be placèd to the view,
And let me speak to th' yet-unknowing world
How these things came about. So shall you hear
Of carnal, bloody, and unnatural acts,
Of accidental judgments, casual slaughters,
Of deaths put on by cunning and forced cause,
And, in this upshot, purposes mistook
Fall'n on th' inventors' heads. All this can I
Truly deliver.

FORTINBRAS

Let us haste to hear it,
And call the noblest to the audience.
For me, with sorrow I embrace my fortune.

I have some rights of memory in this kingdom,
Which now to claim my vantage doth invite me.

HORATIO
Of that I shall have also cause to speak,
And from his mouth whose voice will draw on more.
But let this same be presently performed,
Even while men's minds are wild, lest more mischance
On plots and errors happen.

FORTINBRAS
Let four captains
Bear Hamlet like a soldier to the stage,
For he was likely, had he been put on,
To have proved most royally. And, for his passage,
The soldiers' music and the rites of war
Speak loudly for him.
Take up the bodies. Such a sight as this
Becomes the field, but here shows much amiss.
Go, bid the soldiers shoot.

*Exeunt marching, carrying the bodies, after the which a peal of ordnance
are shot off*

FINIS

HAMLET: 10 TIMELESS LIFE LESSONS

1- THE THIRST FOR REVENGE ONLY LEADS TO OUR SELF-DESTRUCTION

2- KEEP IT SIMPLE. QUIT BEING RHETORICAL AND GIVE SOMETHING OF SUBSTANCE.

"More matter with less art".

3- THINK OUTSIDE THE BOX.

"There are more things in heaven and earth, Horatio, than are dreamt of in your philosophy."

4- WHEN IT RAINS, IT POURS.

"When sorrows come, they come not single spies. But in battalions".

5- INJUSTICE CAN MAKE PEOPLE CRAZY. BUT JUSTICE CAN COST MORE THAN MOST PEOPLE ARE ABLE OR WILLING TO PAY.

6- TALK LESS. LISTEN MORE.

"Give every man thine ear, but few thy voice."

7- ILLUSION IS THE ONLY MEANS TO ACTION. THE ONLY TRUTH IS FOUND IN ILLUSION.

"Stay illusion".

8- PERSPECTIVE MATTERS. LEARN TO ACCEPT LIFE AS IT COMES WITHOUT GIVING JUDGMENT.

"There is nothing either good or bad, but thinking makes it so."

9- DREAM BIG.

"We know what we are, but we know not what we may be".

10- CHOOSE TO BE.

Made in the USA
Las Vegas, NV
22 September 2021